Glass rained down on Darcy.

Smokey's barking surrounded her. The dog was frantic bouncing around Jackson, who lay on top of her behind the coffee table. He rolled off her but remained close to the floor.

"Stay down. That was most likely a rifle shot from a distance. The shooter might still be in place ready to fire again."

She lay on her stomach and peered into his face. Tense seconds ticked by.

Jackson sat up and reached out, touching his hand to her cheek. "You all right?"

TRUE BLUE K-9 UNIT: BROOKLYN

*These police officers fight for justice
with the help of their brave canine partners.*

Ever since she found the Nancy Drew books with the pink covers in her country school library, **Sharon Dunn** has loved mystery and suspense. Most of her books take place in Montana, where she lives with three nearly grown children and a hyper border collie. She lost her beloved husband of twenty-seven years to cancer in 2014. When she isn't writing, she loves to hike surrounded by God's beauty.

Books by Sharon Dunn

Love Inspired Suspense

Broken Trust
Zero Visibility
Montana Standoff
Top Secret Identity
Wilderness Target
Cold Case Justice
Mistaken Target
Fatal Vendetta
Big Sky Showdown
Hidden Away
In Too Deep
Wilderness Secrets
Mountain Captive
Undercover Threat

True Blue K-9 Unit: Brooklyn

Scene of the Crime

Visit the Author Profile page at Harlequin.com for more titles.

SCENE OF THE CRIME

SHARON DUNN

LOVE INSPIRED SUSPENSE
INSPIRATIONAL ROMANCE

Special thanks and acknowledgment are given to Sharon Dunn for her contribution to the True Blue K-9 Unit: Brooklyn miniseries.

LOVE INSPIRED® SUSPENSE
INSPIRATIONAL ROMANCE

ISBN-13: 978-1-335-72191-4

Scene of the Crime

Recycling programs
for this product may
not exist in your area.

Love Inspired
22 Adelaide St. West, 40th Floor
Toronto, Ontario M5H 4E3, Canada
www.Harlequin.com

Printed in U.S.A.

Thou art my hiding place; thou shalt preserve me
from trouble; thou shalt compass me
about with songs of deliverance.
—*Psalms* 32:7

For my counselor and king, comforter and friend, Jesus.

ONE

Brooklyn K-9 Unit officer Jackson Davison opened the back of his SUV where his partner, Smokey, was crated. Eager to work, the chocolate Lab wagged his tail and jumped down at Jackson's command.

Jackson studied the arch of Grand Army Plaza and, beyond that, Prospect Park.

"Let's go find a body," he said. Trained as a cadaver dog, Smokey was part of the Emergency Services Division for the recently formed Brooklyn K-9 Unit.

Jackson clicked Smokey into his leash and took off at a jog toward the memorial. The vendors around the arch were still selling food, though the crowds were smaller than earlier in the day.

A call had come into Dispatch that someone had seen a body in a cluster of trees not too far from the arch. The caller had not identified him or herself and had hung up before giving any details.

Jackson and Smokey ran toward the trees that bordered the entrance to the park. The botanic garden was closed for the day but plenty of people rested on the lawn and utilized the paths as the sky turned gray on this cool September evening.

The leash remained slack. Smokey hadn't alerted to anything, though he kept his nose to the ground. The call could be a total hoax, Jackson knew, but the K-9 Unit would of course respond. The nature of the call bothered him. From the information the dispatcher had given him, the caller had not stayed on the line or provided any information other than a vague location. If the call was genuine, why not identify yourself and why hang up?

Smokey kept his nose on the path as they passed joggers, bicyclists, couples pushing baby strollers. With a jerk on the leash, Smokey veered off deeper into the trees. Jackson's heartbeat revved up a notch. Smokey had picked up on something.

Jackson commanded Smokey to sit so he could unclick his leash. He patted the Lab on the chest, the signal that he could let his nose do its thing. "Find."

Smokey took off into the deep brush and

through more trees. The Lab could find remains that were years old and buried. Most civilians didn't want to think about the five stages of smells of a body after death or the different types of odors Smokey was trained to detect. Tonight would be easy for the Lab, given it was a body above ground. Jackson had no idea how long it had been in the park or the state of decomposition. Or even if there was a body.

Jackson focused on how finding bodies often gave loved ones closure in tragic situations. It wasn't a job for the fainthearted, but it was meaningful. And working with Smokey had brought a renewed sense of purpose into Jackson's life after his breakup with his fiancée.

Smokey disappeared into some bushes where an abundance of gold and red leaves hung on the foliage. Jackson pushed branches out of the way, searching for his partner in the waning light. He could hear the dog moving through the undergrowth, yipping excitedly. They were close.

Jackson caught movement out of the corner of his eye: a face in the trees fading out of view. His heart beat a little faster. Was someone watching him? He could hear people on the paths some distance away, but this part of the park in the deep brush was not where most people wanted to be unless they were up to something. The hairs on the back of Jackson's neck stood at attention as a light breeze brushed his face. Even as he studied the foliage, he felt the weight of a gaze on him. The sound of Smokey's barking brought his mission back into focus.

When he caught up with his partner, the dog was sitting. The signal that he'd found something. "Good boy." Jackson tossed out the toy he carried on his belt for Smokey to play with, his reward for doing his job. The dog whipped the toy back and forth in his mouth.

"Drop," Jackson said. He picked up the toy and patted Smokey on the head. "Sit. Stay."

The body, partially covered by branches, was clothed in neutral colors and would not be easy to spot unless you were looking for it. Plus, it was getting dark. Another hour or so and someone wouldn't see it unless they stumbled over it, which made Jackson wonder how the caller had known it was there.

He keyed his radio. "Officer Davison here. I've got a body in Prospect Park. Male Caucasian under the age of forty, about two hundred yards in, just southwest of the Brooklyn Botanic Garden." He stepped closer to the body and shone his flashlight on it. "Looks like a bullet wound to the chest. We're going to need a forensics team here." It was too much to hope that someone had died of natural causes. Every death was hard for him.

Dispatch responded, "Ten-Four. Help is on the way."

Jackson clicked off his radio. He studied the trees just in time to catch the face again, barely visible, like a fading mist. He was being watched. The person wore a hood that covered part of his or her face. "Did you see something?" Jackson shouted. "Did you call this in?"

The person turned and ran, disappearing into the thick brush.

Jackson took off in the direction the runner had gone. Radioing for backup would slow him down. As his feet pounded the hard earth, another thought occurred to him. Was this the person who had shot the man in the chest? Sometimes criminals hung around to witness the police response to their handiwork. The caller and the killer could be one in the same.

Pulling his weapon, he hurried in the direction the hooded figure had gone, knowing that Smokey would stay with the body.

He came out into an open area where a dozen or so people were having a barbecue and playing guitar and bongos. The revelers stopped their activity and stared at him: a normal reaction to seeing a cop with a gun. Jackson caught a flash of motion in his peripheral vision and resumed his pursuit. He could hear the watcher in the bushes up ahead though he did not catch a glimpse of him. He came out on a path that was mostly deserted. Several runners disappeared over a hill and then he was by himself.

Jackson tuned his ears to the sounds around him. The wind rustling the dried leaves on the trees, music and voices in the distance. He studied the trees in sectors, not seeing any movement. His attention was drawn to a garbage can just as an object hit the back of his head with intense force. He swayed and blinked. Pain radiated from the base of his skull. He heard metal tinging as something was thrown into the garbage can and then the pounding of retreating footsteps. He crumpled to the ground and his world went black.

Minutes or hours later, he didn't know which, his eyes fluttered open and he winced at the bright light shining in his face.

"Hey, there," said a singsongy female voice.

Jackson shaded his eyes. "Get that thing out of my face."

The flashlight was clicked off. "Sorry, I was

checking your pupils to see if they were dilated."

He kind of liked the voice. It reminded him of the nonjudgmental woman who gave directions in his truck GPS. When he'd first moved to New York two years ago, from Texas, that voice had been a comfort as he'd tried to navigate a new city.

He looked up into her face with his eyes still half closed, fearing another dose of blinding light. Soft eyes, blond curls and dimples. Only the forensic suit and booties gave her away. She looked more like a kindergarten teacher than a tech. He'd seen Darcy Fields, the forensics specialist, at a distance when she came into K-9 headquarters or to work a crime scene, but he'd never talked to her.

She leaned back, resting on her knees. "You're the officer who called in the body, right?"

"How did you find me?"

"It took some coaxing—he didn't want to leave the body—but your dog led me to you, and the gathering crowd was a good hint." She turned slightly so he had view of Smokey. Sitting obediently, his tail did a little thump on the ground when Jackson looked at him. And then Jackson saw the gathering crowd around him.

His cheeks grew warm and he stood. Now

he felt stupid. How had he managed to let himself get knocked unconscious? He'd never hear the end it from the rest of the K-9 team.

She held out hand for him to help him up. "I'm Darcy Fields, Forensics."

"I know who you are." He pointed to her paper bodysuit. "The outfit gives it away."

She laughed. "Believe it or not, I was at a very fancy shindig when I got the call." She unzipped her suit slightly to reveal a sequined dress. "Normally my hair is pulled back when I work, not curly." She had a sort of bouncy bright quality that didn't fit with being a crime tech. "So why were you all the way over here playing Rip Van Winkle?"

"There was a someone hiding in the foliage where I found the body. The person took off running and I chased. I think he or she wanted to make sure I found the dead man, but didn't want to get caught. I think that's why I was hit in the head."

Darcy narrowed her eyes. "But you don't know for sure if the same person you saw in the trees hit you in the head?"

"No, I didn't see who hit me and I never got a good look at the person who was watching me." He knew Darcy must see everything in terms of how it would play in court. She wasn't wrong. His theory was only speculation at this point. "I know we can't draw conclusions until the evidence is examined."

"Right. I don't know anything until the evidence speaks to me," she said. "Could be the person you saw in the trees was the concerned citizen who called it in, could be connected to the crime, could be something else entirely."

Concerned citizen, he doubted it. "I didn't get a good look, couldn't tell you if it was a man or a woman. But I think he or she dropped something in that trash can."

Darcy pushed through the crowd of onlookers and moved toward the garbage can, pulling gloves out of a back pocket. She sorted through a pile of plastic cups and fast-food wrappers before pulling out a small gun. "Okay, now things are getting weird."

Some of the crowd dispersed, having lost interest, while others watched Darcy bag the gun.

"I don't think the person I chased was a concerned citizen. I think he or she was a witness to, or a part of, the crime that led to that man being shot," said Jackson.

"That doesn't make sense. Why leave evidence behind? Are we dealing with the world's dumbest criminal?" Darcy held up the bagged gun.

"Believe me, I've encountered some pretty dumb criminals."

Darcy pursed and released her lips as though she were thinking. "Did you actually see him or her drop the gun in the trash can?"

"No. I thought I heard it as I was losing consciousness." Now he realized how flimsy his story sounded from a legal standpoint. "I know it won't stand up in court. Just because events happened close together doesn't mean they're related."

"This could be from a different crime. We won't know until we get it to the lab." Darcy turned to face him.

Even though his gut told him this was all connected, he saw now how he didn't have any solid evidence to link anything together. All he had was what lawyers would call "circumstantial."

"I have to get back to work." She took several steps and then looked over her shoulder. He liked her smile. "I'm glad we found you. I didn't need another mystery on my hands."

He followed her back to the body, where other techs had already cordoned off an area with crime scene tape. A van belonging to the coroner had driven onto the grass. The coroner and his assistant stood by the vehicle, waiting to approach the body.

Several uniformed officers stood around, as well. Jackson approached one of them and gave his statement about the watcher in the woods and being hit in the back of the head. "I'm not the detective on this case, but I think my being hit is somehow connected to that man's death."

The uniformed officer nodded. "I'll make sure the detective assigned to the case gets your statement."

"I'll file a report about being assaulted." Jackson turned his attention back to the crime scene.

Once the coroner examined the body, the forensic team went to work. After pulling her hair up in one of those hair ties women wore like bracelets, Darcy examined the body while the other two techs combed the area around the deceased man.

Jackson clicked Smokey back into his leash. Still stirred up by the face in the woods and what it meant, Jackson hung back to watch Darcy and the others work, curious as to what they might find.

Darcy took notes and performed a cursory study of the body. The autopsy would reveal more. The victim was dressed in casual clothes appropriate for the time of year. Flannel shirt in grays and browns, tan denim jacket, boots and jeans.

As she stared into the victim's lifeless face,

Darcy said a prayer for him and for the family members who would soon be getting the news of the man's death. "Shot at close range. I'd say maybe a .38," she said aloud.

About a month ago, she'd been in the same park dealing with another person shot at point-blank range. The perpetrator of that crime, Reuben Bray, was now in jail awaiting trial.

Jackson Davison and his cute dog were still hanging around. She felt a little distracted by the K-9 officer's presence. He had a faint accent that suggested he wasn't from New York. Somewhere from the South maybe. Every time their eyes locked, her heart fluttered a little. He was probably just hanging around in a professional capacity anyway. What did it matter if she found him attractive? She had a rule about not dating cops. The last time she'd opened her heart to an officer, he'd only been using her to expedite evidence. As nice as Jackson seemed, she'd vowed to never again fall for a police officer.

She looked at the other tech. Harlan Germaine was an older man with gray hair and a beard, and glasses much too big for his thin face. "Did the coroner pull ID on him?" she asked.

"Man's name is Griffin Martel," Harlan said. "Sorry about you having to leave your night out for this."

"Actually, I was grateful. It was kind of not going anywhere." Her church had decided to have a fancy dress-up night followed by a catered meal for all the young singles in the congregation. "Most men's eyes glaze over when I talk about my work. Guess I should get an interesting hobby, so I have something else to talk about. Don't know why I get my hopes up." She spoke under her breath more to herself than to Harlan. "No one wants to the date the nerdy science girl."

Harlan shook his head. "Don't give up so easily, Darcy." Harlan walked away from the body, eyes studying the ground. "I still don't see any shell casings."

"Even if we don't find any, I say the guy was shot here. Plenty of people in the park. Someone would have noticed a body being dragged or hauled here. There is no way to get a vehicle to this area without raising alarm bells. If he was shot here, the killer must have used a sound suppressor," she noted. "Otherwise someone would have heard the shots and phoned it in much sooner. I can see the early stages of rigor in the face and neck muscles, I would put the TOD at less than three hours ago."

"You know this is about the same area that Rueben Bray shot that guy. Same MO, too, shot at point-blank range," Harlan said.

Darcy had thought of that, too. "Reuben is sitting in a jail cell in Rikers. I'm set to testify at his trial soon." She looked back at the dead man. "I hope we don't have a copycat on our hands."

She tilted her head. The overcast sky hinted of rain. "We better hurry or a bunch of evidence is going to be washed away."

Jackson Davison came to the edge of the crime scene. "Smokey's getting restless. I'm going to take him for a run. I'd be curious to know about that gun."

Focused on her work, Darcy barely looked up. "Sure, I'll let you know once we get the lab results. Fingerprints. How recently it was fired. Who it's registered to…blah, blah, blah. You know the drill."

Jackson laughed.

She liked that he seemed to get her sense of humor.

The team worked on, taking photographs and collecting any possible evidence just as rain started to sprinkle from the sky. The coroner moved in to load the body to be taken in for an autopsy.

She unzipped her suit and took off her booties, handing them over to Harlan to dispose of.

"Need a ride?" Harlan shouted over his shoulder.

"Thanks, I took the subway here. I can take it home if you can pack my gear out." The gear would stay in the forensics van for the next time she got called to the scene of a crime on her day off.

She walked the crime scene one final time, taking mental photographs and making sure she hadn't missed anything that might be important later. It was a practice she'd learned early in her career. Though the team was meticulous in photographing everything, she needed to keep a picture in her head, as well.

"Satisfied?" Harlan asked as he loaded the last piece of equipment into the van.

Darcy nodded. She just wanted to get home and soak in a hot tub. Not so much because of work—she loved her job—but because the church event had been such a disaster. "See you bright and early in the morning."

Harlan gave her a salute before walking away.

The crime scene tape remained in place. Darcy picked up her coat and purse from where she'd set them next to an officer guarding the scene when she'd arrived. She stared at the empty space now that everyone had left. Already her mind was trying to picture the scenario that had brought the dead man here. She looked at these cases as a puzzle to be solved. Right now, she only had a few pieces to work with. "How and why did you end up here, Griffin Martel? What is your story?"

Rain started showering from the sky. It was dark. She shone the flashlight where the body had been one more time, searching for a shell casing. She looked up, aware that she was alone. It was so late that she couldn't even hear people in the park. Most everyone had gone home.

A branch cracked in the trees that surrounded the crime scene. Jackson's story of someone watching the body became foremost in her mind. "Hello, is someone out there?"

She shook off her paranoia. All the same, she turned and walked through the trees at a brisk pace, heading for a more open area. When she got to the path that led to the park entrance, she didn't see anyone.

Darcy stepped toward the crosswalk to cross Flatbush Avenue. Halfway across, bright lights shone in her eyes as the roar of an engine surrounded her. A car was coming straight for her. She ran to get to the other side of the street. The car followed her up on the grass just as a body slammed against hers, taking her to the ground. The car sped past and then peeled out of view.

Off to her side, a dog barked.

"What was that about?" The voice was Jackson Davison's. He rolled away from her.

Her heart was still racing. "I have no idea."

He stood and reached out a hand to help her up. His hand was strong and callused. She stood on wobbly knees, resting her palm against her raging heart.

"Some crazy freak, huh?"

"Yeah, I guess," she said.

"I didn't get a look at the make or model of the car or we could call it in."

Her mind tried to rationalize why someone would try to run over her. "Maybe just a guy who had one too many. I'm glad you were here. That car might have mowed me down." Her hands were still shaking.

"After I took Smokey for a run, I was hoping to catch you or one of the other techs," he said. "See what you figured out."

"Any information we have is preliminary. We'll release official statements when we know more and next of kin has been notified. Your department will get a briefing if it's pertinent." Her voice sounded cold. This wasn't about Jackson. She was being defensive because of what had happened with the officer who had only dated her to move his case along. "I'm sorry. It's just that I need to follow proper protocol."

"I understand," Jackson said. "Guess I'm embarrassed that I let myself get hit on the noggin like that. Just wanted to know if it was connected to finding that body."

"Like I said, we've just started to connect the dots." Darcy studied him for a long moment.

The rain intensified and the few remaining people in the area scattered. He touched her arm above the elbow. "Let's get out of this."

They found shelter underneath a gazebo.

Smokey nestled between them on the bench as they took seats to watch the rain. "Sorry about that," said Jackson. "He gets kind of jealous."

Smokey licked his face and then turned his head and groaned at Darcy.

Darcy laughed.

They stared out at the rain and listened to its symphony on the roof of the gazebo.

"You look nice, by the way," he said. "Sorry you got pulled away from your shindig."

"Thank you."

Jackson seemed like a nice guy, but he was a cop, and that made him off-limits to her. Darcy stared down at the dress she'd paid way too much money for and would probably not ever wear again. The disappointment of the party at church, the crime scene and nearly being mowed down by that car—it all hit her at once. She thought she might cry. "I need to get to the subway. I want to go home."

"You seem kind of shook up. A car coming at you like that can take its toll. How about I drive you home?"

"I don't mind the subway."

"Okay, let us at least walk you to the entrance." His voice was filled with compassion. He clicked the leash on Smokey. "I won't take no for an answer."

As they walked through the rain to the subway entrance, she found herself grateful that Jackson and Smokey were with her. The whole evening had left her out of sorts.

At the top of the stairs that led to the subway, Darcy turned to face Jackson. "Thank you. I will let you know if we find anything once we start combing through the evidence."

Jackson gave her a nod. She watched as he turned with his dog and disappeared into the crowd. As she made her way down the subway stairs, she had the oddest feeling that she was being watched.

She stared around at the sea of faces on the platform. Her heart beat a little faster. The crowd compressed, preparing to board the train. Someone bumped her from behind, setting her off balance. She recovered before she fell. She craned her neck to see who had pushed her. All eyes were looking elsewhere.

The doors slid open. Even as she stepped inside the train, she sensed the weight of a gaze on her.

TWO

Jackson watched from the sidelines as Darcy moved toward a throng of reporters outside the building that housed the forensics lab. Cameras flashed and news reporters pressed in close with microphones. Darcy had texted him that she'd be making a statement about the Griffin Martel murder. He'd appreciated the heads-up.

She was dressed in a navy blue suit, but he noticed that her shoes were pink and red, with colorful leather flowers, and she wore a hot-pink scarf.

Thanks to his ex-fiancée, Jackson noticed things like that. Two years ago, Amelia had wanted to make it as a fashion stylist in New York. Wanting to be supportive of her and her dreams, Jackson had put in for a transfer from Dallas. While they'd lived in separate apartments, they had continued to plan their wedding. The idea had been to stay in New York for a few years and then return to Texas. Five months after the move, she'd informed him she was in love with the photographer she worked with on the fashion shoots. Jackson and Amelia had been high school sweethearts. They'd planned a life together from the time they were sixteen. Even a year and half after their breakup, he didn't think the hole inside would ever heal.

From what Amelia had taught him, Darcy was breaking all kinds of fashion rules. He kind of liked that about her. Though he didn't know the reason why, it was common knowledge that Darcy Fields didn't date cops. That suited him just fine. He was not in the market to get involved with anybody. A friendship with someone who understood the nature of his work would be nice, though.

Darcy pulled a typed statement out of her pocket. She gave Jackson a quick smile that showed her dimples then focused her attention on the waiting reporters.

"The body found in Prospect Park on Monday night was identified as Griffin Martel from Trenton, New Jersey. We still do not know why Mr. Martel was here in Brooklyn. We believe he was lured or lead to the secluded spot in the park and shot at point-blank range. No motive has yet been determined, though Martel did have a record for selling prescription drugs. Detectives are currently interviewing his known associates. Police are following all possible leads. We believe at this point that this is an isolated incident and that there is no reason for people visiting or living in New York to be afraid."

A female reporter pushed her way to the front. "Isn't this murder similar to the murder Reuben Bray allegedly committed? Same part of the park? Same method of death?"

Darcy remained poised despite the reporters moving in tightly around her. "Yes, there are similarities. But Reuben Bray was in a jail cell at the time of Mr. Martel's murder."

A male reporter asked, "Is it possible you put the wrong man in jail and that a killer is still on the streets?"

Another reporter piped up. "Are we looking at a serial killer?"

Jackson clenched his jaw. He hated the fear mongering the press tended to elicit. And he didn't like the way they were treating Darcy.

"No, the evidence on Reuben Bray was solid," she said.

The reporters began peppering her with questions. Because of his movie-star good looks, Rueben Bray had become a sort of media darling.

"Aren't you scheduled to give expert testimony in his trial soon?"

"Isn't it true that there was some controversy around charging Reuben with murder?"

"He was low-level criminal who stole cell phones and purses and then he moved on to murder. Isn't it rare for criminals to change the type of crime they commit?"

From his vantage point, Jackson could see that Darcy was gripping the podium. But her voice remained calm. "Yes, but Mr. Bray's psychological profile showed he was a man who couldn't bear to be humiliated. And the man he killed had done that by chasing him down to get his cell phone back. Please, we are here to talk about the murder of Griffin Martel."

The reporters began to crowd Darcy. She took a step back as they surrounded her, essentially blocking the door to the building.

Jackson couldn't stand it anymore. He swooped in and gathered Darcy in the crook of his arm. "I think Ms. Fields has answered enough of your questions today."

"Are you her protection?" a reporter asked.

"I'm her police escort."

"Why does she need to be protected?" The female reporter trailed behind Jackson and Darcy as he led to her toward his K-9 patrol vehicle. "Ms. Fields, do you know how to do your job?"

Darcy planted her feet, her lips drawn into a straight line.

Jackson whispered in her ear, keeping his arm around her. "Don't react. Just keep walking."

As the reporters crowded toward the K-9 patrol SUV, Jackson led Darcy to the front passenger side. Smokey perched in the back seat in his crate, chin in the air. Smart dog, he knew better than to bark or to get excited by the people surrounding the vehicle.

"Excuse me," said Jackson, pushing past a reporter to open the driver's-side door once he'd settled Darcy inside.

A female reporter with a ponytail and penciled-in eyebrows stepped up to him. "Why is the K-9 Unit involved in protecting a forensics tech?" The reporter leaned a little closer to him. "Aren't you the officer who was hit on the head the night Griffin Martel's body was found?"

The assault had made the news. Jackson was standing so the car door acted as shield between him and the reporters. "I'm not protecting her in an official capacity. I'm doing this as a friend. It's clear to me you guys are looking for a controversy where there is none."

The reporter leaned over the open car door and looked straight at Darcy. "Two men are dead. Killed in a similar way and place. How do we know it won't happen again?"

Jackson shook his head and got into the SUV. He gripped the steering wheel and let out a heavy breath.

"Thank you for getting me out of there. The evidence in the Rueben Bray case was solid. I don't know why they have to stir things up like this."

"'Cause they're reporters," Jackson said.

She glanced over at the journalists mingling outside the building. "I need to get back to the lab."

"It's Friday night and you're going back to work?"

"What can I say? I live on the wild side. Stuff is piled up—I want to deal with it. It's not like I have any place to go."

"What are you working on that is so important that you have to give up your Friday night?"

"That home invasion—double homicide, husband and wife, little girl left alive. Lucy Emery?" Darcy said.

Jackson nodded. "I know the case well. Trust me, those unsolved homicides are of foremost importance to the entire K-9 Unit.

One of our officers, Nate Slater, married Lucy's aunt. They've filed papers to adopt her."

The case hit very close to home for the entire unit. The Emerys had been murdered on the twentieth anniversary of another set of parents' double homicide. Same MO, down to the description of the killer, and a young child left unharmed at the scene. That child Penelope McGregor, and her older brother Bradley, who hadn't been home during the murders, now worked for the Brooklyn K-9 Unit. The team believed they knew who killed the McGregors' parents twenty years ago, but he'd eluded capture so far. They were also pretty sure the recent murders had been committed by a copycat.

"I'd like to close that case, too," Darcy said. "There were fibers left on the doorknob at the Emery house that might contain the killer's DNA—if I can just isolate and extract them."

"You're not going to get back into the lab without being swarmed. You can take a break for dinner, can't you? They should be gone by then." Jackson stuck the key in the ignition.

"Sure. I can phone Harlan and let him know." She pulled her phone from her pants' pocket.

He started the SUV and pulled away from the curb. "I know just the place."

While she phoned the lab to let her tech partner know where she was, Jackson wove through traffic to a great pizza place close to the lab. It wasn't Sal's Pizza, his favorite pizzeria, which was down the street from K-9 headquarters in Bay Ridge, but it came a close second. After looking for a parking spot for ten minutes, he finally found one.

Darcy pressed her phone against her chest. "I hope we're going to Park Pizza. It's my favorite."

"You've gotta try Sal's sometime. But yes. And we can eat in the car since getting a table is rough."

Jackson's dinner choice was purposely informal; he didn't want her thinking this was a date. They walked to Park Pizza, which was brimming, as usual, and stood in line.

They each ordered two slices to go and drinks. Once they were settled back in the SUV, Smokey rested his nose on the back seat making sniffing noises when Jackson opened the crate door so the dog could stretch and be with them while they were parked.

"He looks like he wants a bite of pizza," Darcy said.

"He loves the smell of people food, but he'll only eat out of my hand," Jackson told her. "People food isn't good for him anyway."

With her to-go container resting on her lap, Darcy reached back and brushed the top of Smokey's head. "He's pretty charming, looking at me with those big brown eyes."

She laughed and took a bite of her pepperoni pizza. Smokey moved so his nose was still resting on the back of the seat, but he was closer to Darcy.

"I can feel his breath on my neck." She seemed mildly amused. "He really likes the smell of this pizza."

Jackson petted Smokey's head and then under his chin when the dog came closer to him. "What a good boy!" Smokey licked Jackson's face.

Her phone rang. She stared at it. "It's Harlan." She pressed her talk button and listened. "Okay, have a good time with your wife." Darcy ended the call and stared at her phone before putting it away.

"Sounds like everyone else is calling it a night. Are you sure you want to get back to the lab?" he asked.

She looked at him after taking a sip of her drink. "Jackson, thanks. This was a nice break, but I do want to get back to work. The colder the Emery case gets, the less chance we have of solving it."

When they finished their pizza, Jackson

commanded Smokey to get back in his crate. After latching the door to the crate, Jackson started the SUV. Heading back toward the lab, he noted that the traffic was lighter. It was dark already when he pulled into the empty lot. "Where's your car?"

"I use public transit except when in a professional capacity—less expensive."

"Are you all right with working in the lab alone?"

"I do it all the time." She pushed the SUV door open. "Thanks again, Jackson, for the rescue from the reporters." Darcy seemed lost in thought.

"No problem."

He watched her walk to the outside entrance to the lab and swipe her badge across the sensor by the door so it clicked open. Darcy disappeared inside. It seemed sad to him that such a cute and smart woman was working on a Friday night. But then again, what was he doing on a Friday night? "Streaming a movie with my best friend, right Smokey?"

The dog let out a yip.

He was about to pull back onto the street when he saw shadows and movement. Someone disappeared around the side of the building.

Great. A reporter had waited around and

was now looking for a way into the lab to bother Darcy some more.

Darcy hurried down the hall. Her footsteps echoed on the hard floor. After donning her lab coat, she walked over to the microscope that contained a slide with one of the fibers from the Emery case. The fiber was natural, cotton, probably from a piece of clothing. There had been DNA on the fiber, but it was a minute specimen. To make the sample usable, she'd had to grow it using polymerase chain reaction to make the DNA replicate itself.

She let out a breath. She'd actually explained that process to a man at the church dinner she'd gotten dressed up for and watched his eyes glaze over.

She peered at the lens, feeling a heaviness. This was her life, working alone on a Friday night. Dinner with Jackson Davison had been a brief reprieve even if it had been very informal. Though he seemed a bit guarded, she felt drawn to Jackson's quiet nature. He wasn't a man who talked just to hear the sound of his voice. He chose his words carefully. Maybe this would be the start of a friendship for both of them.

She looked through the lens of the microscope just as an odd pounding noise caused her to lift her head. Was Jackson at the door? The sound was coming from somewhere else. Above her, maybe? The lab was on the ground floor of a three-story building. As far as she knew, the offices above her were a nine-to-five operation. Was someone working late?

She shook her head. Her first thought had been that Jackson had come back to tell her something. Funny how thoughts of him lingered in her mind. He'd have to knock on the main door to get in, though. It locked from the inside.

Darcy walked over to a shelf of textbooks and pulled one down. She suspected the DNA on the fiber was skin flakes. The challenge was that it was such a small sample.

She leaned on the counter and flipped through the book, hoping for clarity on how to proceed. Anything that fell outside of standard lab procedure might be called into question in court. Her mind was always on the little girl who had been in the home at the time of the murders. She was in a secure, loving home now. And if they could catch the man who had killed her mom and dad, she would grow up with a sense of closure and that justice did prevail.

Darcy closed the textbook. The lights in the lab flickered off. Darcy stepped toward the switch, toggling it. But the room remained dark. A breaker must have blown. Holding her hands out in front of her so she wouldn't bump into anything, she moved to the drawer where a flashlight was kept.

A hand went over her mouth. Another wrapped around her waist, holding her arms in place.

Terror raged through her. She twisted to get away, thrashing with all the strength she had. She freed herself and whirled around. This time her assailant attacked her from the front, reaching for her throat. In the process, she was backed into a counter. Her assailant's hold on her remained strong. As they struggled, pieces of evidence and equipment fell to the floor. She tried to pull away from the counters before more work could be destroyed.

She moved with such force that though she broke free from the grip of her assailant, she fell on the floor. She crawled on all fours toward where she thought the door might be. The assailant pushed more things off the counter. Items crashed against the floor. Glass shattered.

Gasping for air, Darcy reached out for a wall and pulled herself to her feet.

A body slammed against hers and she was facedown on the floor again. She flipped over onto her back. Hands wrapped around her neck and squeezed. She clawed at the hands trying to choke her.

"Darcy." A voice sounded in the distance and then she heard footsteps up the hall. The same direction the assailant had come from. The voice was Jackson's.

The hands let go of her. Her assailant crashed toward the door and then retreating footfalls echoed up the hallway. Choking and coughing, she wheezed in air. Another set of footsteps hurried past her in the hallway. That must be Jackson going after her attacker.

She sat up, still in shock from the assault. She reached out for a wall to steady herself, her heart pounding wildly. Her legs felt like cooked noodles, but she pulled herself to her feet. She glanced over her shoulder. Because it was so dark, she was unable to fully assess the damage to the lab.

She made her way to the door.

When she peered down the hallway where the two sets of footsteps had passed, a flashlight shone in her face, coming toward her.

"Jackson?" Her voice was hoarse.

He ran to her. "I tried to catch him. He got away through the main door of the lab on this floor."

"Yes, you can open it from the inside, but it locks behind you."

His hand reached out for her in the dark. "You okay?"

She was still shaking. "What happened? How did that guy get in?" More than the attack, she was upset about the work that had been destroyed by her struggle with the assailant.

"He got down to this floor through the ductwork on the floor above you. I followed him. He accesed the second floor through an unlatched window by the fire escape. I was just getting ready to pull out of the lot when I saw someone sneaking around outside. I thought it was some reporter looking for a scoop."

"No." Tears warmed the corners of her eyes. "Oh, Jackson. He broke things in the lab and then tried to strangle me." Her voice faltered.

He took her in his arms. "Hey, it's okay."

She rested her face against his chest. "I don't mean to be such a basket case."

"You've had quite a shake-up." He held her until she pulled way.

Darcy wiped at her eyes. "I'm going to go look at the breaker box to see if I can get the electricity back on. I have to know how much damage was done. Can I borrow your flashlight?"

"I'll go with you."

She was grateful for his offer. Though it appeared that the attacker had escaped, she was still not calmed down. She moved down the hallway to the breaker box. Jackson shone the light for her while she pushed the breakers back on. Light filled the hallway and spilled out of the main lab.

"Darcy, I have to call this in."

"I know. The attacker might have touched stuff, maybe there are fingerprints." She thought for a moment, trying to remember. "I think he was wearing gloves."

"You can't do the dusting. You're the crime victim."

She let go a nervous laugh. "Yes, of course, that would represent a conflict of interest. Me investigating my own crime."

"Look, the detectives will be here shortly. You can make a statement and then I'll take you home. No way am I letting you ride the subway."

"Jackson, thank you so much. I just need to get my jacket."

She stepped back into the brightly lit lab. The sight of the smashed glass on the floor made her feel like she'd been punched in the stomach. "Oh, no." She moved to pick up an evidence bag with shell casings.

Jackson grabbed her at the elbow. "Don't touch anything."

"Of course. What was I thinking?" She stared at the mess. The attack had thrown her so far off-kilter, she'd almost contaminated the crime scene. A total rookie move. As she stared at the disarray, she still couldn't absorb what had happened. "The stuff on the counter that got pushed off was mostly from some cold cases we're working on. Nothing current. But all the same, it's messed-up evidence."

"It does seem kind of random and angry."

She shook her head. "Who would do such a thing? A reporter just would have tried to corner me and ask me questions."

"Yeah, maybe we can rule them out," Jackson said.

"The list is a mile long of people who don't like the results the lab produces for trials," said Darcy. "Do you think this attack was about revenge or anger?"

"It's clear that someone doesn't want you or the other techs to be able to do your work. But if they wanted to destroy evidence for a specific case, this wouldn't be the way to do it."

"Or they don't want us working on a current case. If you destroy the lab, it slows down our ability to move cases toward trial." She touched her neck where the assailant had tried to choke her. "It would take time for someone to find evidence connected to a specific case. Maybe they thought they were going to have time to look around and didn't count on me being here."

Jackson shook his head. "Hard to say."

A chill ran up her spine. She leaned a little closer to Jackson, relishing the sense of safety she felt when she was close to him but unable to shake the fear that invaded her thoughts.

THREE

Once detectives arrived and took Darcy's statement, Jackson ushered her up the hallway and out the door. She seemed to have regained her composure and now was focused her concern on the lab being processed properly. Maybe thinking about gathering evidence had distracted her from the trauma of the attack. Jackson knew from experience that there could be a delayed effect where Darcy's emotional response was concerned. He wanted to stay with her until he was sure she was going to be okay.

A forensics van from Manhattan pulled up outside. Two techs, a man and a woman, got out.

Darcy watched them enter the building. "Guess that is the outside team who will process the evidence. I know one of them. I would really like to talk to him."

Jackson cleared his throat.

"I know. I know. It's not my case. It can't be. I just hope I can go back to work tomorrow," Darcy said.

"Where do you live?"

"Williamsburg."

"Me, too. Come on, Smokey and I will take you home." Jackson held the SUV door for her and then got in behind the wheel. She gave him the address.

He drove through the city streets, past neighborhoods that were quiet and others where the night had clearly just begun. He circled the block several times before he found a parking space not too far from her apartment building.

"Do you live alone?"

"My sister lives with me, but she is away on an overnight field trip. She's a choir teacher at a private high school."

"How about I walk you to your door?"

Her wrinkled forehead suggested she wasn't crazy about the idea.

"I know you can take care of yourself, Darcy. This is for my piece of mind and, besides, Smokey needs to stretch his legs. There was no time to get him out of the crate when I was chasing the intruder. He would have gotten some exercise then."

"Well, I can't deny Smokey some exercise."

They got out of the SUV and headed up the block toward her place.

Smokey emitted a low-level growl.

"What is that about?"

"I'm not sure," Jackson said. "Something's bothering him."

She placed the key in building's entrance lock but didn't turn it.

Darcy took her hand away from the door, leaving the key in the lock. The hesitation suggested she was concerned about entering her building. Smokey's agitation had given them both pause.

"Why don't you let Smokey and I go inside and clear your place?"

She nodded.

He was glad she wasn't brushing off safety concerns. "You stand back. Let me open the door."

Darcy stepped to one side while Jackson turned the key in the lock and opened the door. Her apartment was on the ground floor. As he opened the door to her place with her key, she said, "The light switch is just on the inside of the wall."

He felt along the wall, flipped on the light and then commanded Smokey to enter and search. "Stay in the hallway for now," he told Darcy.

Smokey circled the room, sniffing the couch and the overstuffed chair. The dog padded into the kitchenette but never alerted.

Darcy's apartment was done up with furniture that looked like it had come from thrift and antique stores, albeit repainted in bright colors. She had a lot of antique-looking, floral-printed curtains and pillows, and he noted a tablecloth and doilies. The whole room looked like a place his grandmother would like, only more vibrant.

Smokey came and sat at Jackson's feet. "Looks like it's all clear."

"I suppose that's good news." Darcy untied her scarf, tossed it over the back of a chair, kicked off her shoes and flopped onto the couch. "At least I can catch my breath."

Maybe, Jackson thought, Darcy had been at the wrong place at the wrong time and the attack was about revenge against someone else or destroying evidence. But then he thought about the car that had tried to run her over near Grand Army Plaza. He was concerned about her safety. He really didn't feel comfortable leaving her. Darcy struck him as being a very independent woman. She probably would rebuff his offer to protect her.

He sat on the opposite end of the couch. Maybe he could keep the conversation going.

"So why do you think that person was in the lab tonight?"

She closed her eyes and thought for a moment. "It has to be the attack was about something the lab did, not me personally. Somebody didn't like results that sent someone to prison." She put her hand on her hip. "We've already talked about this, Jackson."

Maybe she'd figured out he was trying to delay leaving her. "True. I'm just trying to figure it out."

"The destruction of the evidence seemed kind of random," she said. "I think it is someone mad because our work sent a loved one to jail. That would be my guess."

A scratching noise made both him and Smokey jump. Jackson stood.

"That's just Mr. Tubbs, my cat. He wants out. He must have been hiding when you cleared the room." She disappeared down the hall.

"Sorry about that. I must have shut the door after I cleared the room. He was well hidden for Smokey not to alert to his prescence." Jackson hadn't realized how on edge he was until the noise of a cat put him on high alert. Smokey picked up on his nervousness and paced. As partners, they were tuned in to each other just as he would be if with a human officer.

Darcy emerged from the hallway, a fat gray

cat plodding behind her. "Don't worry, Mr. Tubbs likes dogs."

Jackson moved toward the Lab and commanded him to sit. "Smokey has been trained to deal with all kinds of animals." Homing in on the cat, the dog thumped his tail on the hardwood floor and emitted a whine.

Mr. Tubbs, acting as though he had not even seen Smokey, jumped up on the couch. The feline did not so much as rest on the arm of the couch as he draped himself. His round body made his legs appear stubby.

"So do you want a cup of tea or something?" Darcy asked.

"That would be nice," Jackson said. She must have sensed his reluctance to go but wasn't going to push him out the door.

"Go ahead and sit down." Darcy busied herself in the kitchenette, pulling things out of cupboards and putting the kettle on.

Jackson again settled on the couch, away from Mr. Tubbs. Still sitting, Smokey watched the cat intently. The cat flicked his tail and narrowed his eyes.

Darcy took her seat on the couch, saying, "It will take a minute for the kettle to boil." She turned to face him. Her light brown eyes were full of life. "I appreciate you being worried about me, but I'm okay here. I'll lock my door and windows. I always do."

Jackson rose to his feet and shoved his hands in his pockets. He wandered across the room where one wall was a floor-to-ceiling book-shelf. In addition to the science, chemistry and crime detection books, Darcy also had books on art and some classic literature. "I've read a lot of these books. Grew up in the country with no television."

"Jackson, you're avoiding what I just said."

He ran his fingers though his hair. "Look, Darcy, I know you can take care of yourself, but I think maybe Smokey and I should at least do a quick search around the building."

"Then will you feel comfortable going home?"

The answer to that question was no, but he nodded all the same.

"Do the search. The tea will be ready by then."

"Lock the door behind me. I'll knock three times when I come back." He wasn't sure why he felt protective of her. It certainly wasn't be-cause she acted like some kind of damsel in distress. Maybe he was starting to have big brother feelings toward her. He missed his sib-lings in Texas. Since his breakup with Amelia, he hadn't gotten out much to meet new people.

His idea of a social outing was basketball with the other K-9 officers. Maybe it was time to change that.

Darcy rose. "Okay, I'll wait for your knock."

Jackson clicked the leash on Smokey and headed for the door.

Once outside the apartment, Jackson waited for the sound of the dead bolt clicking into place. He then left the building, searched the side streets, circled the building and then took Smokey up the stairwell. Smokey didn't growl. The September night was dark and crisp. Several streets away, he heard the thrum of Friday-night traffic but the streets around Darcy's place were pretty quiet.

Satisfied, Jackson returned to Darcy's door and knocked three times.

Darcy slid back dead bolt and undid the locks.

"All clear," he told her as she opened the door.

She seemed mildly amused by his protective nature.

He nodded.

"Tea's hot."

"Great, I'll have some and then Smokey and I will be out of your hair."

She handed him a steaming mug. "You haven't been bad company." He liked her smile. Those dimples really got to him. "It's not like I had a crazy night planned. Just hanging with Mr. Tubbs and a good book."

"Yeah, it's pretty much the same for me and Smokey."

"Well, we should do something about that." She took a sip of her tea. "As friends, I mean. I don't date cops."

"Yeah, I heard." He turned toward the window by the door that looked out on the street where the residents of the building probably parked.

She stood beside him. "You asked around about me?"

"It's sort of common knowledge." He shrugged, feeling his cheeks grow warm. "That policy is all right by me."

He took another sip of tea. Behind him, Smokey became suddenly agitated. He emitted a high-pitched bark. Jackson turned to look at the dog as a percussive boom hit his eardrums. Glass shattered all around him. Taking Darcy down with him, he dove for the cover of the coffee table.

The last thing he heard was Darcy's scream.

Long, straight shards of glass came at Darcy. Fueled by some primitive survival instinct, she'd taken a step back right before the booming sound vibrated through her chest. Glass rained down on her. Smokey's barking surrounded her. The dog was frantically bouncing around Jackson, who lay on top of her behind the coffee table. He rolled off of her but remained close to the floor.

"Stay down. That was most likely a rifle shot from a distance. The shooter might still be in place, ready to fire again."

She lay on her stomach and peered into his face. Tense seconds ticked by.

She noticed that her hand was bleeding. The sight of the blood did not bother her, but she was suddenly aware of the pain of the cuts.

Jackson reached out, touching his hand to her cheek. "You all right?"

She nodded, unable to form words.

A voice came at her from the side. "What happened to break your window like that? I was up the block when I heard it. I phoned it in, Darcy."

It took her a moment to realize the man staring at her through her shattered window was her upstairs neighbor, Mr. Blake. He was an older, hunched-over man who wore a wide-brimmed hat all the time.

"Thank you." Her voice sounded like a child's voice.

Jackson said from beside her, "Sir, get down

and out of the way. We think someone shot the window out from across the street."

Mr. Blake's eyes grew wide with fear and he stepped out of view.

Jackson lifted his head and peered through the shattered window at the high-rise building across the street. "The shooter must have scouted the area, got into place and waited for you to stand in front of the window."

The high-rise was mostly offices with some eateries on the ground floor. All the windows were dark. "Long-range rifle. Maybe four or five stories up," Darcy said. "I wonder what caliber bullet the shooter used."

Jackson's forehead furrowed.

"Thinking about the tech part of a crime calms me down." She looked around, taking in her surroundings. The damage was largely to the window. Mr. Tubbs, she noted, had disappeared like the smart cat he was.

She heard sirens in the distance.

"Smokey and I are going to search that building across the street. Maybe the shooter is still around. You stay back and down low."

Jackson and Smokey headed out the door and across the street.

Within minutes, the flashing lights of the police, fire department and ambulance filled the street.

Jackson returned, shaking his head. Whoever had shot at her had gotten away. He came to stand facing her.

He reached up to touch her forehead. "You have a cut there."

His touch was warm on her skin. For some reason, she wanted him to hold her. Silly. She shook her head and took a step back. Maybe it was just because the shooting had frightened her. "I'm sure the EMTs can fix me up."

They were ushered out to the ambulance. Smokey trailed behind them. Harlan and the other members of the forensics team arrived. Darcy knew it would not be appropriate for her to work the scene. But that didn't mean she couldn't ask questions. Harlan approached her. "I heard about the lab break-in. We might not be able to work tomorrow."

She nodded and Harlan jogged away to join the rest of the team.

A patrol officer wandered over to ask them questions about what had happened as an EMT cleaned and bandaged her cuts. The were sitting inside an ambulance, the warmth of the blanket the EMT had offered her giving Darcy some comfort. Still, she felt like she was shaking from the inside.

Jackson got to his feet, throwing off his blanket. "I see glass in Smokey's fur." He combed his fingers through the dog's coat. "I'll need to brush him when I get home." Smokey remained still.

"I'm so sorry that happened. He's such a good dog."

"It's not your fault, Darcy," he said. "All of it's just another day at work for him."

Jackson ran his hand over Smokey's sleek, dark head and then under his chin.

Mr. Blake walked over to her. "I talked to the super. He can order replacement glass in the morning and they can start the install, but you'll have to find someplace to stay for tonight."

"Thanks, Mr. Blake, for doing all that." She watched as the old man wandered back toward the growing crowd of onlookers.

"Do you have a place to go?"

"No place close," she said. "I have relatives in Connecticut. I don't feel comfortable calling a friend at this late hour. I suppose I could get a hotel room."

"Given the nature of this attack, I don't think you should be alone." Jackson turned back toward the broken window. "You can stay with me. I have a roommate, but we could set up an air mattress on the floor. The couch isn't too bad to sleep on, either."

Darcy clutched the blanket at her neck. She

didn't have a lot of options here. "I'm not sure what to do."

"Between me and Smokey, you'd be safe for the night. Maybe we can talk the department into providing you with some protection." Jackson took a few steps away from the ambulance and then ran his fingers through his hair. He seemed hesitant to say what he wanted to say. "It's clear now that this isn't directed at the whole lab. Someone is upset about something you've done, probably connected to your work."

Jackson had vocalized the thought that had been spinning through her mind. The attacks were personal. There was nothing in her private life that warranted this level of violence. She barely had a private life. It had to be over a case she'd worked or was working. As the spokesperson for the Brooklyn forensics unit, she'd gotten used to dealing with attacks and accusation from the press, but this was a whole new ballgame. "This is getting serious, isn't it?" She took in a deep breath to summon up some courage.

A Bible verse came to mind.

I can do all things through Christ who strengthens me.

"If it helps with your decision, no expectations are placed on my offer other than friendship and keeping a colleague safe."

"Give me a minute to make sure Mr. Tubbs has water and food for the night. He's used to being shut in the back room, so he won't be able to jump out the broken window. I'll throw some things in an overnight bag and text my sister to let her know what's going on." She studied Jackson for a long moment. His features softened as he met her gaze. "Then we can head over to your place."

A few minutes later, Darcy was buckled into the passenger seat as Jackson drove through the mostly dark residential streets. She rested her head against the seatback, feeling the fatigue in her body. "Do you think whoever attacked me meant to kill me or is it just anger that is boiling over?"

Jackson kept his hands on the wheel as he looked straight ahead.

As she thought about the nature of the attacks, his silence told her everything she needed to know.

Someone wanted her dead.

FOUR

Even though it was his day off, Jackson awoke early to let Smokey out into the fenced yard and put the coffee on. Darcy slept on the couch, partially covered by the quilt one of his sisters had made. One of her legs stuck out as she slept on her side, turned away from the back of the couch. Blond hair fell over her face.

His roommate, who worked in finance, had gotten up even earlier than he had and left for the day. Jackson tossed a load of laundry in, let Smokey back inside and started to break some eggs for breakfast before Darcy stirred. Smokey munched his food in his bowl.

There was no wall between the kitchen and the living room. Darcy sat up, stretching her arms and yawning.

"Hey, you want some coffee?"

"Sure."

"We're not in a hurry this morning," he said, reaching for the coffeepot. "It's my day off and I doubt the lab is going to be accessible just yet."

"Harlan texted me. They are taking the most pressing evidence over to the Manhattan lab, but they're backed up, too. Everything is at a standstill for now. It will be at least a day before they will let any of the techs in to fully assess how much damage was done to the cases we were working on." The tone of her voice suggested frustration.

He poured her coffee and brought it to her. She took the mug, wrapping her hands around it while the steam swirled up.

Jackson beat the eggs he'd broken in the bowl and poured them into the sizzling frying pan. "Hope you like scrambled eggs with green peppers and onions."

"That sounds delicious." Clutching her coffee, she rose and wandered toward the living room window.

Jackson spoke in a calm but intense voice. "Darcy, get away from the window please."

Her face blanched as fear clouded her features. "Sorry, I forgot." She stepped back and wandered into the kitchen, which had only one small window above the sink.

"Didn't mean to upset you. We just can't take any chances."

"No, I get it." Her voice was somber.

If the memory of last night was enough to make his chest feel like it was in a vise, he couldn't imagine how it had affected Darcy emotionally. Though he was impressed with how well she held herself together.

He tossed the veggies into the frying pan and moved the eggs around with a spatula. Offering to set the table while he cooked, she searched cupboards for plates and pulled silverware from the drawer.

They sat across from each other. Darcy took several bites of the scrambled eggs. "This is really good. Thank you."

"You're welcome." Jackson liked that she enjoyed eating his cooking. She didn't seem like the kind of woman who would order a salad if they went to a steak house together. Now why had he thought of that? Amelia had always eaten like a bird.

Smokey wandered over to the table and rested his chin on Jackson's leg.

"He really wishes he could have some eggs." Amusement danced through her words.

Smokey wagged his tail.

Jackson leaned closer to his partner. "You need to stick to your dog food, buddy."

"He is charming," said Darcy.

Smokey turned his head toward Darcy and wagged his tail.

"He likes you. He doesn't respond to everyone that way," Jackson said.

She reached out and stroked Smokey's head. "That means I've made two friends."

They ate for several minutes without talking.

Darcy took the last few bites of her eggs. "I feel a little lost today. I can't go to work. And I doubt I can go home. Even if they've cleared the scene, it will take time to replace that window in my apartment."

He met her gaze across the table. That sweet, welcoming face with the light brown eyes just never seemed to fit with the level of scientific knowledge she displayed. He liked the contrast. Darcy was a person with depth and interest. "It's my day off. Smokey and I were headed over to Dog Beach in Prospect Park. But I don't feel comfortable leaving you here alone."

"That makes us both prisoners," she said. Her full mouth curved up into a soft smile. "I appreciate you wanting to make sure I'm not attacked again."

"You got me figured out, don't you?"

"I don't mind. Yesterday was a bit much. And I am concerned." Her shoulders jerked up to her ears and then she leaned toward him. "I can call Mr. Blake to see if they have pulled the crime scene tape away. If they have, I'd like to get my laptop. I would be able to access some of the current files so I can start narrowing the list of people who might have something against me."

"Sure, we can do that."

Light danced through her eyes. "Your accent comes out just a little bit. Texas, I'm guessing."

"Good guess. Been here two years, you'd think I'd manage to sound a little less like a country boy."

"I kind of like it." She took a sip of coffee.

They finished breakfast and washed the dishes together.

Darcy made her phone call. "Mr. Blake said the window installer has been delayed, but the crime scene tape is gone. So I can at least check on my cat and grab my laptop."

"Okay, I'll take you over there."

While Darcy was in the bathroom, Jackson made a call to ask about permanent protection for Darcy. As expected, he got the usual story about how stretched thin the regular police units were, and that the amount of paperwork involved and level of bureaucratic hoops he'd have to jump through made him wonder if it would just be easier for the K-9 Unit to informally protect her.

Darcy emerged from the bathroom with her blond hair pulled back in a ponytail. She wore capris, a blouse and jacket and canvas shoes imprinted with cats.

Jackson loaded Smokey into the back of his crew cab truck and Darcy got into the passenger seat.

They drove through Williamsburg, Darcy seemingly lost in thought.

"I wonder..." she said. "That night you and Smokey found the body in the park...and that car that came after me. Maybe it wasn't random."

A chill skittered across his spine. "I suppose the list of relatives who vowed revenge over the years for your testimony putting one of their relatives in prison is pretty long. Someone could have seen the forensic van and looked for you."

"I've gotten my share of hate mail. It doesn't help that I'm the spokesperson for Brooklyn forensics. We shouldn't assume it's a case from the past. It might be a current case, maybe someone is afraid of what I will find, or it could be a case that is about to go to trial."

Traffic slowed and then stopped all together. Jackson looked in his rearview mirror. Though he did not want to alarm Darcy, a compact car seemed to be following them.

As traffic came to a standstill, Jackson seemed to tense up. Darcy's stomach tightened in response to his change of mood.

They were on a street that had lots of coffee shops and places to eat. She watched the people on the street, focusing in on a woman who looked to be about her age. The woman was with a man who had a baby in a backpack-style baby carrier while she pushed a stroller with a second child.

"I used to think that was going to be me by now."

Jackson followed her line of sight. "They look like a happy family. Why can't it be you?"

"I'm twenty-nine." She shrugged. "It's hard to meet people when all you do is work." She shook her head. "My sister is two years younger than me and she's engaged."

"You never know. Everyone operates on a different timeline."

"How about you?" Darcy asked. "Have you met anyone?"

He tapped his hands on the steering wheel. "I was engaged when I transferred up here. We moved so she could get ahead in her job. We found separate places to live and were making wedding plans. We talked about going back to Texas once she got some experience." His words seemed tainted with intense emotion. Hurt or maybe even anger? Jackson looked through the windshield, focusing on some faraway object.

Smokey emitted a small whine from the back seat.

Dogs, she knew, tended to pick up on the emotions of their owners, so she reached out to pet him. "My question upset him, didn't it?" She spoke in a whisper.

Smokey licked her face.

Jackson glanced over at her. "Look, there is just no point in bringing up the past. It's all behind me. I've come to love this city. I found a great church. I love my dog. I have a good life."

So he wasn't going to tell her any more about what sounded like a past-tense relationship and some deep hurt. That was okay. As a friend, Darcy knew enough not to push. "I hope the window installer shows up soon at my apartment. I appreciate your hospitality, but Mr. Tubbs shouldn't spend too much time alone, and I miss my little place, my kitchen, my bed, my reading chair."

"Do me a favor when you do get to go back to your apartment. Stay inside and keep the doors locked until we can get a handle on who did this and why."

Her stomach twisted into a knot. She knew Jackson was making the suggestion because he wanted her to be safe, but being a prisoner in her own home would only prolong the ordeal. "I'll stay away from the windows and keep the curtains drawn, but I'm not going to hide. The sooner I can figure out who is behind the attacks, the sooner this will be over. I am aware of the danger, but I intend to be proactive about this."

He stared at her. A faint smile made his eyes light up. "Well then, I reserve the right to check in on you...as your friend."

She studied him for a long moment. The sun shining on his brown hair brought out the coppery strands. His eyes were a light green. She hadn't noticed that before. "You may do that...as a friend."

Traffic started to inch along again.

After they'd driven for several blocks, he checked the rearview mirror and then the side one. In the back seat of the crew cab, Smokey stood.

Darcy tensed. "Something's up."

"Just paying attention." He turned to her and winked. "It's my job, remember."

She craned her neck. Smokey licked her face, blocking her view in the process. The dog seemed nervous. Even if Jackson was good at hiding his emotion, his partner gave everything away.

"Smokey is not so sure about that."

Jackson released a single chuckle. "Okay, I give up. There's a dark-colored compact car behind us. Sorta blue, sorta black. It has been behind us almost from the time we left my house. I've noticed it twice when I checked my mirrors. A couple of cars back, same lane. Don't look behind you, use your mirror."

Darcy tilted her head to look into the side mirror. She had a view of just part of the car.

The light turned green, but traffic was still moving very slowly. Jackson switched lanes without signaling and then made a tight turn down a side street. She waited a moment before checking to see if the car had followed. "I don't see it."

Jackson took several more turns.

"Could be nothing," he said after a long silence. "Traffic is really slow. I'm wondering if there wasn't an accident or a construction job that went sideways. Now that I have taken all these detours, I'm thinking it might just be faster to get on the expressway."

"I'm with you," she said.

He inched forward until he could turn onto a street that led to the expressway. Traffic whizzed around them as they merged into the flow. A florist delivery van erratically changed lanes several times. At one point, she had a view of the driver as he pulled into the lane next to them. He was clearly talking on his phone.

"That guy makes me nervous."

"Me, too," Jackson admitted.

The van slowed until his front end lined up with the bumper of Jackson's truck, then pulled in behind them. All around them cars changed lanes or surged ahead. She glanced through Jackson's side window. The small car off to the side looked like the one they'd seen earlier. She zeroed in on it, trying to get a look at the driver.

Metal crunched against metal. The florist's van hit them from behind. Before she could recover, there was another bump, this one more intense. Her body swung forward and then slammed back against the seat. The truck jerked and the scenery whirled around her in flashes of color as Jackson's truck seemed to be flying and twisting through space. Her only clear view was of the guardrail looming large in Jackson's window.

Jackson gripped the wheel, his jaw like granite, eyes focused straight ahead. The truck vibrated and skidded at the same time. Brakes squealed. More metal bent, crunched, scraped against something. Her view was of the van, then a red car, then Smokey slamming against the seat.

The crew cab stopped moving. Other vehicles gave them wide berth as they sped around the truck, which was braced against the bent guardrail. Another vehicle, a delivery truck, faced them, its front bumper lying on the pavement. Darcy had no memory of having hit the delivery truck. It must have spun around in the process.

Her body felt like it had been jarred and shaken.

Jackson had already clicked out of his seat belt and was crawling in the back to check on Smokey.

A moment later, she heard sirens in the distance. She looked around, not seeing the florist's van or the little compact car anywhere.

FIVE

Jackson's heart was still racing as he reached over and touched Darcy's shoulder. Her face had drained of color and her gaze was unfocused. "Are you okay?"

She nodded. "I'm still breathing, and I don't think anything is broken…if that's what you mean."

He gave her shoulder a squeeze before turning his attention back to his dog.

Jackson made soothing sound as he ran his hands over Smokey's fur. The dog seemed okay physically but was extremely agitated.

The flashing lights of police cars and other first responders surrounded them. A man approached the truck and knocked on Jackson's window.

It took Jackson a moment to realize it was Tyler Walker, a detective with the Brooklyn K-9 Unit. If his cognitive processes were that messed up, there was no denying that the collision had affected him. Jackson was a strong man mentally and physically. The thing that had him the most shaken was how the accident had endangered Smokey and Darcy.

Jackson rolled down the window.

"You three okay? I happened to be in the area running down a lead and recognized your truck," Tyler said.

Jackson nodded. "I don't think anyone has any broken bones."

"Why don't we get the EMTs to check you out, and I'll give you a ride. Looks like your truck is going to need to be towed."

As Tyler yanked open the driver's-side door, Jackson said a quick thank-you prayer that another member of the team had been so close by.

Both Darcy and he had to crawl out the driver's side of the truck because the passenger door was pressed against the bent guardrail.

As he exited, Jackson assured Smokey that he would return. The dog offered him a half-hearted tail wag. "We got to get him to the vet," Jackson told Tyler, "just to make sure there is no internal damage."

"No problem. He can ride with Dusty." Dusty was Tyler's K-9, a golden retriever who specialized in tracking. "Why don't you guys go get checked out? Smokey should calm down once he's in the SUV with me and Dusty."

Uniformed police were already taking measurements of skid marks and photographs. Another officer was talking to the driver of the delivery truck.

Darcy walked beside Jackson as they made their way to the ambulance.

"It was a florist's van that caused the accident," she said. "Both the woman in the compact car and the van driver were on the phone. What if they were talking to each other?"

Once again, Jackson was impressed by Darcy's keen powers of observation. "We can't prove that until we track down one of the drivers and can get a warrant to get a look at their phone." He hadn't been able to get a read on the dirty license plate; most of it was obscured. The compact car was a popular make and model all over Brooklyn and would be impossible to track down by description. "Do you remember what florist it was?"

"No, but I would recognize the logo if I saw it."

The EMT, a slender man probably in his early twenties, stepped toward them. "You folks were in the accident?"

Jackson turned his attention to the EMT. "I think we're both okay, but we can't take chances."

The EMT eyed Darcy and then Jackson. "Did either of you hit your head?"

Both shook their head.

"And neither of you is in any pain?"

"Just kind of shaky," Darcy said.

"I'll look at you first," the EMT said.

Darcy sat inside the open ambulance. Jackson pulled his phone out and searched for "Florist Brooklyn." As each businesses came up on the screen, he showed it to Darcy until they found one with a logo that matched the van she'd seen.

Once Jackson was checked out and delcared okay, they got into the SUV with Tyler. Dusty was in her crate in the back with Smokey.

Tyler dropped them off at headquarters, which was right next to the K-9 training center and veterinarian. On the way over, Jackson had called Gina Mazelli, the resident vet, to let her know they were bringing Smokey over.

With Smokey in tow, they entered the veterinary clinic and were led into an examination room. An exam table was situated in the center of the room. Counter space containing equipment and medical supplies took up most of three walls. The fourth wall had a small desk with a computer and a file cabinet.

Gina called out from an adjoining room

where the yipping and yapping of puppies could be heard. "Be with you in just a second."

Darcy bent over to pet Smokey's back.

"Gina's living in the training center temporarily as a sort of foster mom," Jackson told her. "One of the other officers found a German shepherd a few months back who'd just given birth," said Jackson.

"I heard about Brooke. She had five pups, right?"

"Yeah, how did you know?"

"Officers talk when they bring in evidence for me. Brooke caused quite a stir when they were finally able to bring her in. Officer Lani Jameson told me."

Gina poked her head through the door. Her red hair was pulled back in a ponytail. She held a puppy in one arm. With her free hand she pushed her silver-framed glasses back on her nose. Gina always reminded Jackson of his older sister. Melody was a champion barrel racer and a cowgirl to the core, but what always got Jackson was her big heart. She would take in any kind of stray from a houseplant to a horse with a bum leg. Gina Mazelli was the same way.

"Let's get Smokey on the exam table," Gina said.

The veterinarian's wrinkled forehead told

Jackson that something was stressing her out. The puppy in her arms, he noted, seemed listless and looked to be half asleep. The puppy licked Gina's forearm.

"Everything okay?" he asked.

"It's Maverick. She's having digestive issues again," Gina said.

Darcy stepped forward. "I can hold her while you examine Smokey, so you don't have to put her down. I'm sure that is scary for a puppy who is not feeling very good." *

Gina's expression brightened. "Thank you." She handed the puppy over to Darcy who put Maverick's belly against her chest while she stroked her back.

Jackson lifted Smokey onto the exam table.

"So you said he was in a car wreck?" Gina stroked Smokey's ears.

"Yes," Jackson said. "I'm sure he got slammed around on impact."

Gina pressed her hands on Smokey's belly, watching his reaction. "We should probably do an X-ray just to make sure no bones are fractured. He wouldn't necessary be yelping in pain over that." She probed each of his legs then glanced over at Darcy.

Maverick was wagging her tiny tail and licking the underside of Darcy's chin.

"Looks like somebody made a new friend," Jackson quipped.

"She's sweet," Darcy said.

"I don't suppose you'd be interested in baby-sitting tonight?" Gina asked. "I have to be with my grandmother through some surgery she needs. I don't have anyone to cover the night shift with Brooke and her pups for me. With Maverick still kind of touch and go, I don't feel right leaving them alone."

"Well, I'd like to, but I'm not an expert on dogs or anything," Darcy replied.

"I can stay with them, too," Jackson said. Given the accident, he didn't want to leave Darcy alone and, even if her window was fixed, he didn't think it was a good idea for her to go back to her apartment.

Gina glanced at Darcy and then at Jackson. "Between the two of you, you should be able to handle it just fine."

Maverick grunted.

"I'll go get Smokey x-rayed. If you want to, see if you can get Maverick to eat something and keep it down. Her food is in the next room, the soft stuff. She's used to being hand fed." Gina disappeared into an adjoining room with Smokey.

Darcy and Jackson took Maverick into the room where Mama Brooke was settled with her four other puppies. They all appeared healthy and energetic as they crawled on mom and played with each other in the pen.

Jackson found the shelf that contained soft puppy food. Darcy sat in a chair that was covered in dog hair, though she didn't seem to mind. Her focus was on Maverick.

Jackson handed her the dish. She dipped her fingers into the food and placed them close to Maverick's mouth. "Come on, sweetie, you've got to eat."

Jackson stroked Maverick's head with a single finger. "Come on, girl."

The dog nestled against Darcy but didn't take the food. "I'll just hold her for a minute and then we'll try again. Poor little thing. I hope she makes it. I always root for the underdog."

"Me, too," Jackson said.

A glow had come into Darcy's cheeks as she'd looked down at the puppy. Jackson felt himself drawn to her in a deeper way. The level of compassion she showed for the little fighter of a puppy moved him. He liked the size of Darcy's heart, too. "You'll be a good mom someday."

"Puppies and babies are two different things. Besides, I just don't see any sign of a husband anywhere."

"You never know," Jackson said.

She shrugged. "My sister will probably make me an auntie in a couple of years after she gets married." Darcy drew the puppy even closer to her. "Maybe that is supposed to be my role in life." She lifted her gaze to look at him. "I'm glad you're my friend, Jackson."

He felt a surge close to his heart. There was a part of him that wanted to be more than friends with Darcy. He let go of the thought almost as quickly as it had entered his head. He reached out to pet the puppy. His fingers brushed over her hand. "Yes, it's been good for both of us."

Maverick licked her fingers where there was still food residue.

"Let's try one more time." Jackson dipped his fingers into the food dish and placed his hand close to Maverick's nose so she could sniff first. Then he brushed her mouth with the food. This time the dog licked it up.

"There you go, little one." Darcy's voice was filled with joy.

"You two make a good team." Gina stood in the doorway, Smokey beside her.

They both turned to look at Gina.

From where she lay inside the pen, surrounded by puppies, Brooke thumped her tail and whined. Smokey trotted over to the pen.

"Smokey checks out. No fractures or anything," Gina told Jackson. "He's good to go."

"Great then," he said. "We've got some police work to do."

"I'll see you guys tonight then. I'm sure Maverick will be glad to see you, too," Gina said as she reached her arms out to take the little dog.

Darcy gave Maverick a kiss on the head before handing her over.

As they stepped back into the reception area, Jackson phoned Gavin Sutherland, the sergeant of the Brooklyn K-9 Unit. He explained the situation about the accident and Darcy maybe being able to identify the driver of the florist's van. "I'm without a personal vehicle right now and I would like to treat this as official police business."

"No problem," Gavin said. "You can use your K-9 vehicle. Also, I'll ask around—one of the other K-9 officers probably has a beater car you can borrow until your truck is out of the shop."

"Thanks for doing that," Jackson said.

"Bear in mind that Darcy is technically a civilian. Keep her safe."

Jackson glanced at Darcy, who was twirling a strand of her blond hair and studying a piece of lab equipment on the counter. "No problem."

"Let's send another unit with you just to be on the safe side. I'll find out who's available," said Gavin.

Jackson, Darcy and Smokey left the veterinarian's and headed over to the parking area where a few of the K-9 vehicles were kept. After securing Smokey in his crate in the back of an SUV, Jackson got behind the wheel.

He offered Darcy a smile and a pat on the shoulder as she got in on the passenger side and buckled up. "Let's get this done."

"Yes," Darcy said, letting out a heavy breath. "So I can get on with my life and work."

Jackson hoped that would be the case.

Darcy could feel her stomach twist into knots so tight it almost hurt. She pressed her hand against her belly. It was scary to think she might soon be looking at the man who had attacked her and then run her off the road and maybe even had gone after her in the park when she left the crime scene. She said a prayer of thanks that Jackson and Smokey were with her. She wasn't sure what the woman in the compact car had to do with anything.

"So where exactly are we going?" Jackson asked. "I need to GPS the address."

Darcy paged through the information about the florists on her phone. "It looks like they have several storefronts throughout Brooklyn, but they get their flowers from the greenhouses at Brooklyn Nurseries." She came to pictures of the interior and exterior of several greenhouses. Vans like the one that had caused Jackson to wreck his truck were parked in a gravel lot by one of the greenhouses. "I think our best hope would be to go to the greenhouse. The delivery vans must do their pick-ups there, and it looks like they are parked there at the end of the day." She recited the address to him.

"Sounds good. I know where that is." Jackson keyed the radio to talk to Dispatch. "We're headed to the greenhouses off New York Avenue. Sergeant Sutherland said he'd send another unit."

"Detective Walker is back in that area now. I'll have him meet you there," the dispatcher said.

"Ten-Four," Jackson responded. He stared through the windshield of the SUV and sped up.

"Wow this is pretty big," Jackson said as they neared the entrance to the nursery.

"The ad said 20,000 square feet." It looked like there were enclosed greenhouses and well as some outdoor plant areas. The delivery vans were parked in the lot in front of the third greenhouse, just like the picture had shown.

They pulled into the gravel lot where Tyler Walker was already parked. He stood outside his vehicle, Dusty on a leash.

The knot in Darcy's stomach grew even tighter as she pushed open the passenger's-side door and stepped down.

Jackson and Smokey came to stand beside her as she stared at the delivery vans. There were no people inside the vans or around them. "He might be out on deliveries."

"Maybe, but we've got to start somewhere," Jackson said.

Tyler stepped over to them. "Dusty and I will go have a look at those vans. There might be paint residue from your truck. Do you remember what part of the van hit your truck?"

Both of them shook their heads.

"We were hit from behind," Jackson said.

Tyler trotted off with Dusty in tow. Every time Darcy saw Tyler and Dusty together, she thought about that saying that owners looked like their dogs. Tyler's blond hair was the same color as the golden retriever's fur.

Jackson peered inside the greenhouse. "Looks like there is someone in there watering plants. Let's go describe the guy to her to see if she knows who we're talking about."

"Okay, but the description will be kind of basic. Like I said, if I saw the guy, I would know that it was him."

The greenhouse worker looked to be a woman of about forty. She wore a straw hat and baggy coveralls and a checked shirt. She filled a water can up from a spigot, smiling when Jackson and Darcy came toward her. Her gaze rested on Smokey for a moment. "Can I help you?"

"I'm Officer Davison from the Brooklyn K-9 Unit. Are you in charge around here?"

The woman nodded and held out her hand to Jackson. "I'm Lynn Costello, the owner."

"We're looking for one of your delivery drivers who may have been involved in an accident earlier today."

The woman put down her watering can. "Are you saying one of my drivers left the scene of an accident?"

"We don't know anything for sure. We just need to question the man." Jackson turned to Darcy. "This woman was involved in the accident. She saw one of your delivery trucks and the driver."

Jackson was doing what police officers did best, trying not to raise alarm bells so the suspect wouldn't be warned and have a chance to bolt.

Darcy stepped forward. "He had short dark hair, sort of shiny. Medium build. He had on a blue shirt."

The woman straightened and wiped her forehead with the back of her hand. "All the drivers wear the blue shirts. And you are describing at least three of the guys who do deliveries for us."

As Darcy had feared, finding the driver would not be straightforward.

"Are any of the men who fit that description here right now or due to return anytime soon?" Jackson asked.

Darcy appreciated that he wasn't going to give up easily.

"The drivers pick their stuff up early in the morning and then are out for most of the day. Unless, for some reason, we don't have the usual number of orders. I'd have to check, but think all the trucks went out full this morning."

"But there are trucks sitting over by that other greenhouse," Jackson noted.

"You know, I'd have to check the log to find out if someone came back early. Don't recall any of the trucks looking like they'd been in a crash. I don't pay that much attention to the delivery trucks coming and going. I'm in the greenhouse some of the time and in office the rest of the time." The woman picked up her watering can with a jerky motion, indicating that she was becoming a little irritated with Jackson's questions. "Some of those trucks need repairs and others are for overflow days."

Jackson pulled a business card out of his shirt pocket. "We'd like to question the three men who might match this woman's description." He pointed at Darcy.

The woman took the card and put it in her shirt pocket. "If one of my drivers left the scene of an accident, that is a serious offense. I just can't believe one of them would do that."

Jackson pulled out a notebook and pen. "Could you give me the names of the three who fit the description we gave you?"

"Joe Donnelly, Angus Graft and Spencer Fisher."

"Thank you so much for your time," Jackson said.

"If you will excuse me, I have a great deal of work to do." After grabbing her watering can, she turned and walked down one of the aisles that contained rows of pink carnations.

Darcy and Jackson turned toward the entrance of the greenhouse. A single pink carnation lay on the dirt floor of the greenhouse. Jackson reached down and picked it up. He handed it to Darcy. "It's your color."

Her cheeks warmed. "Thank you." It was

such an impulsive thing to do but, for some reason, receiving a flower from Jackson, even one that had probably fallen out of a bouquet, made her heart flutter. If only he wasn't a police officer, she could see herself wanting for them to be more than just friends.

They stepped outside. Detective Walker and Dusty stood some distance away by their vehicle. He shook his head, meaning he hadn't found anything.

Jackson shook his head, as well. Both officers loaded their dogs into the K-9 vehicles before getting in behind the wheel.

Jackson turned to face Darcy. "That wasn't a dead end. We've got some names to go on."

She still held the carnation. "I know. I'm not giving up."

Jackson turned the key in the ignition and looked over his shoulder to check behind him.

Darcy looked through the windshield. Detective Walker had already pulled out onto the street when a delivery van pulled into the parking lot with the other vans. She could just make out the man behind the wheel as he reached to open the door and get out. He had black hair.

"That's him," she said. "That's the man who caused the accident."

SIX

Jackson snapped his head around in time to see the driver, who had just arrived, slam his door shut and hit the gas. The van's tires spat up gravel as he peeled toward the street, swerving around Tyler's vehicle and almost hitting an oncoming car.

Jackson turned and headed out after the speeding florist's van. Tyler must have deduced that something was up because he sped up, as well.

Tyler slipped in front of the van and Jackson pulled up to its side in an effort to box him in and force him to stop. The driver of the van did a sharp turn off the street. Jackson noted the sign that said Wingate Park was within blocks, cranked his steering wheel and followed, pressing the gas. The van headed toward the park but veered off the street and drove over the grass past a racquetball court. Alarmed park-goers scrambled to get out of the path of the van as Jackson followed it onto the grass.

Staying on the street, Tyler did a wide arc with his vehicle, trying to head the van off once it got on the other side of the park. The van dipped down into a culvert but didn't come up the other side. Either the guy had stalled out his motor or he was stuck.

Jackson stopped his vehicle. Having seen from the street what happened, Tyler moved in closer still in his SUV.

The van driver spun his tires for only a few more seconds before the door popped open and he stumbled out. He took off running across the park toward a cluster of trees where a car could not go.

"Looks like the chase is on." Jackson pushed open his door. "Stay here, Darcy, lock the doors. He might be armed."

Smokey barked from the back.

Tyler drove across the grass toward the stalled-out van then stopped and unloaded Dusty from the K-9 SUV. Because Dusty was a tracking dog, she would pick up the scent that the panicked suspect left in the air. Though Smokey wasn't trained to track, he'd still be able to follow Dusty's lead. He would be a help apprehending the suspect. The sound of a barking dog was often terrifying enough to make a suspect give up rather than be taken down by a K-9.

When the two officers with their K-9 partners made an appearance, the people close by scattered to other parts of the park.

Jackson and Tyler headed for the trees where the driver had disappeared. Dusty put her nose to the ground and picked up the suspect's scent almost right away. Because he was in a heighted state of fear from being chased, the delivery driver emanated an odor in the air that was like a map to a dog trained to track. With the dogs leading the way, they hurried through the trees and brush.

As they ran, Jackson caught flashes of blue in the trees. The noises of the delivery driver hurrying through the foliage reached Jackson's ears from time to time. Smokey ran ahead of him as Tyler and Dusty drew farther away, still on the same parallel path. He lost sight of the fugitive, but the wavering tree branches told him they were still headed in the right direction.

He could hear the rush of traffic as it sped by on the street. A reminder that the city still surrounded this oasis of greenery.

"Let's split up," Jackson shouted. "Smokey and I will try to flank him to make sure he doesn't get over to that street to flag down a ride." Or worse, hold someone at gunpoint. Because they still didn't know if the suspect was armed or not, they had to assume he was.

Tyler and Dusty veered in the direction that led straight through the trees.

Jackson commanded Smokey to come back to him then the two of them took off running. He saw the driver pass by the concert grandstand before he ran back into a cluster of trees. Jackson radioed Tyler about the location. His feet pounded the hard ground as Smokey kept pace with him. The dog was used to running. He frequently heeled at Jackson's side when he jogged.

Off to his side, Dusty's barking grew fainter and then louder.

Jackson scanned the trees, not seeing any blue or hearing any movement that was human. He kept running toward the edge of the trees as the sound of traffic droned in his ears. They were getting close to the street. His goal was to get to the street before the fugitive did. Dusty would be coming at him from the other side.

Smokey emitted an intense bark, indicating he'd seen something. Jackson heart pounded as he came to a stop. His K-9 stood beside him but did not sit. He barked three more times. Jackson followed the direction that Smokey indicated. Though it was nearly drowned out by the sounds of the busy street and surrounding city, he could hear but not see someone moving through the brush.

Unsure of Dusty and Tyler's location, he commanded Smokey to "Find" and they took off at a sprint.

Up ahead, Jackson could see the driver running toward the street. The suspect had shed his blue shirt, apparently thinking the brown shirt underneath would not contrast as much with the foliage.

The man was only feet away from the street.

Once he was clear of the trees, Jackson pulled his weapon. "Police! Hold it right there."

Smokey stood his ground, but the twitching of his body indicated he was ready to take the man down if commanded.

The man's eyes grew wide. He moved as though he was going to surrender but then dropped to the ground and rolled back toward the trees.

That was unexpected.

"Get him," Jackson commanded and Smokey surged ahead. Jackson returned his weapon to his holster and sprinted after the dog.

Dusty's barking had faded. Jackson wondered if the K-9 had lost the scent. The loss would be temporary. Dusty was among the best tracking dogs he'd worked with. The suspect had likely doubled back and was headed toward the racquetball courts. He and Tyler should be able to flank him and take him down before he had a chance to get away.

Jackson's heart pounded as he hurried through the brush, trying to put a visual on Smokey.

He didn't see Smokey. Fear that something had happened to his partner or a civilian made him run even faster. He pumped his legs as his strides ate up the ground.

He saw movement in the trees and pulled his weapon. Dusty and Tyler emerged.

The detective shook his head. Dusty put her nose to the ground. Once she recovered the scent, both officer and partner headed along a park trail.

Jackson shouted a command for Smokey to return to him. The dog didn't show up. He stood, listening, hoping. His heart squeezed tight.

Come on, Smokey, where are you?

A surge of adrenaline flooded his body and he ran even faster, hoping to spot Smokey.

The foliage at his side rustled. He turned and raised his gun. Smokey emerged, wagging his tail and hanging his head.

Relief flooded Jackson. "So glad to see you, buddy." Another stronger scent must have crossed Smokey's path to cause him to go off track. "Let's get back to work." He tried to sound stern, but gratitude laced his words.

"We've got a job to do, come on," Jackson said. Still not sure which direction to head, he turned in a half circle.

Smokey growled. The dog had either smelled or heard something.

"Lead the way. Let's go."

Smokey hightailed it through the brush, back toward the stalled van.

Jackson heard Dusty barking and then an enraged voice. "Call the dog off right now or she gets it!"

Jackson's heart squeezed tight as he sprinted even faster. Did the delivery driver have Darcy?

Tyler said something in a low voice and the barking stopped. With Smokey by his side, Jackson hurried to the edge of the trees and peered out. Fear seized his heart. The driver must have tried to jack the K-9 vehicle where Darcy had been waiting. The driver's-side window was broken. He must have smashed it to get access, then grabbed Darcy as a hostage. As he stood beside the SUV, the driver had one arm wrapped around Darcy and held a knife to her neck.

Jackson glanced from side to side. Some people were off in the distance, but there were no other civilians in harm's way.

Tyler held his weapon on the driver but spoke in a calming voice. Dusty had come to his side when she'd been called off. The dog's body language, though, suggested a high level of agitation and a readiness to take the suspect down on command.

Jackson couldn't hear the words. Darcy's face was pale, and her expression was strained, but she seemed to be holding it together. She, too, spoke to the driver, her tone suggesting she was trying to convince him to let her go.

"Shut up! Shut up both of you," shouted the driver. "I'm taking the car and I'm taking her with me as an insurance policy. Gimme the keys or she's dead."

Jackson pushed past the rising panic and guilt over Darcy being dragged into this. There was no cover that would allow him to move toward the driver without being noticed. He couldn't risk Darcy's life by commanding Smokey to go after the suspect. Smokey would have a stretch of ground to cover before he could get close enough, allowing too much time for the driver to use the knife.

Faced with nothing but bad options, he raised his gun and stepped out into the open. "You heard the lady, drop your weapon and back off."

* * *

Darcy could feel the pressure of the knife against her neck. Her heart pounded and she struggled to take a deep breath. The delivery driver's other arm dug into her stomach where he held her, so she couldn't get away. With a knife pressed against her skin, she dared not even try.

All the same, a sense of calm washed over Darcy when Jackson and Smokey stepped out of the trees and he pointed his gun at the driver. Her body was tensed up. She was still afraid for her life, but seeing Jackson renewed her hope that this wasn't the end for her.

"Both of you back off. I'm getting in that police car and she's coming with me."

The driver's tone had switched from rage to fear. That wasn't necessarily good news. A fearful man was just as likely to kill as an angry man.

"Look, we know you caused the accident with my truck earlier." With his weapon still aimed at the man, Jackson took a step toward him.

"You don't want additional charges against you, do you?" Tyler added.

"You got two officers with guns trained on you," Jackson pointed out. "What do you think your chances are of getting out of here alive?"

The man let up some of the pressure of the knife. His resolve was weakening. "It wasn't me. She offered me money," he said.

Darcy wondered if he was referencing the woman in the compact car, the one that had been following them right before the accident.

"We can talk about this," Jackson said. "Just toss the knife and let the woman go."

She could hear the man take in a breath. He must still be considering his options. The moment filled with tension.

She said a quick prayer. *God, please help all of us to stay alive. Including this man.*

"Please, let me go," Darcy whispered.

The driver tightened his grip around her stomach. Both Smokey and Dusty looked ready to jump the man and take him down if commanded to do so. The guy must realize the possibility for escape was not good. He might be able to use the threat of hurting her to prevent the officers from coming close to the police vehicle before he drove away. But he must know he wouldn't get far even if he did escape.

Darcy had to prevent him from taking her in that car. If he was backed into a corner and saw no escape, he might just stab her. There was no way she could free herself from his grip and get to safety before he used the knife.

Darcy looked to Jackson, hoping her expression communicated that she was wondering what to do.

"Stay right where you are, Darcy. He knows he's out of options." Jackson softened the tone of his voice as he told the guy, "You said yourself this wasn't all you. Let the woman go."

"Drop the gun and back away," Tyler said.

The seconds stretched out. Darcy could hear her own heartbeat thrumming in her ears. The driver was breathing so heavily that his exhale was like puffs of wind against her cheek.

The man let go of Darcy and pushed her forward. She heard the thud of the knife falling on the ground. She rushed toward Jackson as relief flooded through her body. Knowing that Jackson had to focus on the suspect, she stepped out of the way.

As he and Tyler moved in, Jackson winked at her.

Her heart was still pounding as she watched Jackson cuff the man.

"So somebody put you up to this?" Tyler asked.

"A woman called me when I was on the expressway and offered me money to ram a truck. I don't know how she got my cell number."

"Did she pay up?" The man had been bent over the hood of the SUV while Jackson cuffed him. Gripping the cuffs, Jackson pulled him upright, so he had to straighten.

"Yes, but I didn't see her. She asked me where my next delivery stop was. The money was waiting for me in an envelope," the driver said.

Interesting. So it was confirmed—whoever was behind the attacks was a woman. The attempt to run her over, the shooting at her apartment, the attack in the lab. Her attacker had been very strong, but it had happened so fast. Then again, if the woman was willing to let this driver do her dirty work, maybe someone else had been hired to attack her in the lab.

Tyler stepped up to the suspect. "I can take him in my car since you need to transport Darcy," he said to Jackson.

"Sounds good." Jackson patted Tyler on the shoulder and then turned his attention to Darcy. "You all right?"

She nodded but then tears streamed down her face. "I guess I was pretty scared." She felt a torrential flow of emotion that had been at bay while her life was under threat. She wiped the tears away.

"Anyone would be," he said. "You handled yourself just fine."

She knew she needed to process what had happened to her by talking about it. "At first, when he held the knife on me, he just wanted me out of the car so he could take it, but then when Dusty came toward him, he grabbed me."

"Let's take you back to the station. You can file a report."

"We need to make sure we get that guy's phone," Darcy said as Jackson opened the passenger door for her. "We might be able to trace the woman who put him up to this through the call she made." The phone had probably already been ditched or was a throwaway in the first place, but every avenue of investigation needed to be explored. "And we'll find out where he picked up his payment. The woman might have been caught on camera." She was talking a mile a minute because she was still worked up from having been held at knifepoint.

While Jackson loaded Smokey into his crate, she closed her eyes and rested the back of her head against the seat.

Jackson got behind the wheel and buckled his seat belt. He placed his hands on the steering wheel but didn't turn the key in the ignition. "It was scary for me, too. I know you were the one with a knife to your throat, but I don't know what I would have done if I'd lost you. I shouldn't have put you in that kind of danger."

"Don't feel bad. You left me in the safest

place possible. You had no way of knowing that guy was going to double back like that."

He smiled at her. "All the same, I like being your friend. I don't want to lose you." He turned the key. "Let's go get your statement and then I'll take you back to your place. I'm sure there is stuff you want to get for tonight when we watch the pups."

"Yes, I need to pick up some things, including that laptop I never got." She rested her palm against her chest. Her heart still hadn't slowed down. "I miss my apartment and my cat, but I don't want to put my sister in danger. I wish this was over with."

"Me, too." Jackson put the SUV in gear. "We'll see if the detectives can get any more information out of that driver."

"You think he was telling the truth, that he never saw the woman who paid him to cause the wreck?"

"I do, actually," Jackson admitted. "The guy was really scared." He turned to look at the broken driver's-side window. "Looks like my K-9 vehicle is going into the shop, too."

"At least now we know that it is a woman who is behind the attempts on my life. That narrows down the possibilities," Darcy said. "Once I have my laptop, I'll be able to access some of my cases."

Jackson headed toward K-9 headquarters.

There was no safer place for her than to be with Jackson and Smokey, but Darcy knew until she figured out which case had caused someone to desire her dead, it was just a matter of time before there would be another attempt on her life.

SEVEN

After they dropped the K-9 patrol vehicle with the broken window off at a shop that serviced all the vehicles, they waited for a replacement car. Gavin Sutherland and Lani Jameson showed up in separate K-9 cars, leaving one for Jackson to use. They drove to Darcy's place to get the laptop.

As they pulled into Darcy's neighborhood, Jackson tensed. If the woman in the compact car was lying in wait anywhere, it would be at Darcy's apartment. He circled the block several times, finding a space that required them to walk several blocks out in the open and cross the street. Smokey walked between him and Darcy.

He stared up at the building where the shooter had probably been watching Darcy's place, waiting for a chance to shoot at her when she stood in front of the window. Had their suspect done the shooting herself or had she hired that out, too?

They crossed the street. The window had been replaced in Darcy's ground-floor apartment and the curtains were drawn. Darcy slowed, her features growing taut.

Jackson placed a supportive hand on her back. "Smokey and I are right here with you."

Darcy twisted the necklace she wore, clearly nervous. "I texted my sister that I'd be by. She's not home right now, but she said Mr. Tubbs was fine." She pulled her keys from her purse.

"We should maybe call your neighbor to see if he noticed anyone suspicious hanging around here today. What was his name, Mr. Blake?"

She nodded. "That would be a good idea. I don't want to spend too much time here."

The little waver in her voice revealed how afraid she was. She might be reliving the shooting, as well. He knew from experience that it took a long time to heal from a trauma like being shot at. As a police officer, getting shot at was just part of the job. But Darcy was used to being tucked away with her samples and microscopes.

She turned the key in the door lock and gripped the knob. He touched her arm. "Why don't we let Smokey go in first? You stand at the apartment door and I'll stand behind you while Smokey has a sniff around."

"Good idea." She pushed the door open and stepped inside. Jackson closed the door behind them. His hand wavered over his gun.

They walked the short distance to her apartment door. Jackson commanded Smokey to go inside. Mr. Tubbs, who was lying on the couch, jumped down and sought the safety of a window ledge. Smokey moved through each of the rooms and then returned to sit at Jackson's feet.

"If you want to give me Mr. Blake's number, I'll call him while you get your laptop. Smokey has given us the thumbs-up that no one is in here, but I'll be right behind you all the same."

"My laptop is in the bedroom," Darcy said then recited Mr. Blake's number.

"Let me make the call first."

Once Mr. Blake picked up, Jackson identified himself. "Have you noticed anyone or anything strange since Darcy's window was shot out?"

Mr. Blake cleared his throat. "A woman who said she was a friend of Darcy's stopped me on the street this afternoon. She asked if I knew when Darcy would be back."

Jackson's heart skipped a beat. "And she wasn't someone you had seen around here before?"

"No."

"Can you describe her for me?"

"Shoulder-length brown hair. Kind of a muscular gal. Not old, probably thirty or so."

That could be a third of the women in New York City. "Nothing distinct about her?" Jackson asked.

"No, not really. Can't say as if I would recognize her if I saw her again. Just talked to her for a couple of seconds."

"Thank you, Mr. Blake." Jackson ended the call.

Darcy twisted the pendant on her necklace. Something Jackson realized she did when she was nervous. "So she was here asking around about me, huh?"

Tension wove through his chest. None of this made him feel any better about Darcy staying here. Even if her sister was around. At least she'd be safe tonight. "Let's go get your laptop."

Darcy headed down a hallway toward her bedroom. Jackson and Smokey followed her.

She picked her laptop up off the quilt on her bed. She hesitated for just a moment, glancing out her bedroom window. The curtains had not been drawn.

He caught movement outside the window. "Darcy, get down." Something thudded against the wall outside her bedroom.

Still holding the laptop, she fell to the floor by her bed.

Smokey barked.

Jackson drew his weapon and pressed his back against the wall by the window. He angled his head so he had a view of the sidewalk and the apartment building across the street. The only people on the sidewalk close to Darcy's place were two kids kicking a soccer ball. That must have been what had made the thudding noise.

"All clear," he said. "Guess we are both just a little on edge."

She rose to her feet. "That's an understatement."

They returned to the living room and Darcy grabbed a book and some snacks, placing them in a bag along with her laptop. She petted Mr. Tubbs. "I'll be home soon, big guy."

They stepped outside. While Darcy double-checked to make sure the door was locked, Jackson and Smokey headed outside to watch the street and surrounding buildings.

The street by Darcy's bedroom was a quiet one, but the one her living room faced was a busy thoroughfare at this hour. Though it had been quiet the night Darcy had been shot at, it was bustling with activity now. People were coming home from work and headed out to dinner.

Staying on high alert, he walked close to Darcy as people brushed past them on the sidewalk. He watched Smokey's reaction, knowing that his hackles would go up at anyone he perceived to be a threat. He opened the car door for her and waited before loading Smokey in the back. He continued to watch the traffic behind and around him as he headed to Bay Ridge and the K-9 Unit training center, where he and Darcy would babysit Brooke and her pups for the night.

He didn't relax until he and Darcy were inside the training center with the doors locked. In the veterinary clinic, Gina had left a note explaining about giving medication to Maverick and the feeding and care for the other puppies and Brooke. Gina instructed them to check on Maverick through the night and to call her if the condition worsened. The dogs were in a pen in the training center.

Darcy found a fold-out chair in one of the storage closets. "Did Mr. Blake say anything helpful in narrowing down who might be behind the attacks?" There was also a rocking chair in the corner of the training center that was likely used when holding the puppies. It looked like the one that had been in the veterinarian's area.

"Not in appearance. Mr. Blake's description was kind of generic. Brown hair and in good shape. He did say he thought the woman was probably around thirty years old."

"That is helpful. I can eliminate any of the older women connected to cases I worked." She got her laptop out and flipped it open. She clicked several keys. "I need to call Harlan to jog his memory at some point. It occurs to me that someone I put away and who's now out might want revenge. My work hasn't sent that many thirty-something women to prison. We can check my list against recent parolees."

Darcy seemed less afraid when she could focus on catching the woman who was after her.

While Darcy worked on her laptop, Jackson played with the other puppies and then held Maverick. The training center had both an indoor and small outdoor area for the dogs. He took Smokey and the puppies outside while Brooke remained close to Maverick. When he returned with the puppies trailing behind him, Darcy was still busy on her laptop.

"Find anything?"

She leaned back in the chair and rubbed her eyes. "I've come up with five possibilities. Once I have access to the files on the computer at work, the list will get longer." She glanced down at Maverick as the other puppies raced toward their mom. The pup still looked kind of listless. She closed her laptop. "Maybe I should hold Maverick for a while if you like. I don't think she's up for any rough puppy play."

"Sure, why don't I order some takeout?" He reached down to pick up the puppy and hand her to Darcy.

"Chinese sounds good. Anything from the Dumpling House would be great," she said.

Jackson dialed the number and wandered away from the noise of the puppies so he could place their order.

He walked the floor, coming to stand at a window. While he spoke on the phone, he separated the blinds just a tiny bit to peer out. It was dark outside though the streetlights did provide a level of illumination. A person in a hoodie leaned against a pole. Jackson could only see the individual from the side. He couldn't even tell if it was a male or female. A chill skipped up his spine as he was reminded of the watcher in the woods the night he and Smokey had found Griffin Martel's body.

He knew Brooke would need to go for a long walk later since she needed more exercise than her puppies. That would give him an opportunity to make sure no one suspicious was hanging around the training center.

After placing his order, he clicked his phone off and turned around. Darcy was sitting in the rocking chair, holding Maverick. "When the take-out comes, it might be a good idea for you to stay out of sight and let me get the door," he told her.

She nodded, drawing the puppy closer to her chest. "I get why I have to do that. It doesn't mean I have to like it." Maverick let out a whimper. "She doesn't like it, either."

"I'm glad you have a sense of humor about this." Jackson walked over to her and stroked the puppy's head.

They sat and visited until there was a knock on the outside door.

Darcy got up and retreated to a back room. Jackson called Smokey, who walked beside him as he moved to answer the outside door. A police officer in uniform with a K-9 would probably be enough to intimidate anyone who had violence on her mind.

Knowing he had to be ready for anything, Jackson had not removed his shoulder holster with his police-issue Glock. He knew the woman behind the attacks wasn't above hiring muscle to help her and every attempt on

Darcy's life had, up to this point, come out of nowhere.

Jackson took in a breath and reached for the doorknob.

Darcy sat on the floor, holding Maverick while she listened to Jackson interact with the delivery person. The other puppies played at her feet. All of them had followed her.

Though she understood Jackson's reasons for making her hide, it felt like the very thing she was trying to prevent was happening. The attacker was calling the shots on her life. She would be a virtual captive until this woman was caught and put behind bars. Darcy had never been one to back down from a challenge, but she was battling a sense of defeat over the whole thing. She had to do something.

With Maverick still resting in her lap, she pulled her phone out and texted Harlan.

Any chance we will be able to go back to work tomorrow?

She heard the outside door close and Jackson's footsteps, along with the patter of Smokey's paws, coming toward her. Jackson appeared, holding a brown paper bag. His smile lifted her spirits.

"Not sure where the most sanitary place is to eat, considering the whole place is dog central," he said.

Darcy stood, still holding Maverick. "Probably Gina's desk in the clinic. We can wipe it down." She lay Maverick in her little separate bed carefully. The puppy licked her hands as she drew back.

It took only a few minutes to find some disinfecting wipes and another chair for their makeshift dinner table. Jackson sat kitty-corner to her as they both pulled containers from the bag. Darcy checked the contents of several boxes before choosing the sweet-and-sour chicken.

"I hope you like what I got." Jackson spooned some rice onto his paper plate.

"Looks like you got the special sampler of a bunch of different things on the menu. It's what I always order from that great place near the lab." After spooning out half the chicken, she handed him the take-out box.

"Do you order from them a lot?"

She nodded. "They're our go-to place for not only lunch but late nights at the lab. My sister and I order from them quite a bit, too, since my apartment isn't far from the lab." She opened several more boxes and put the food on her plate before settling in to enjoy her meal after they said grace.

Something about sharing a meal with him felt very comfortable. Smokey lay down at Jackson's feet.

When she smiled at the dog, he thudded his tail against the floor. "He doesn't act very hungry."

Jackson looked at his dog and smiled. He scooped up a big bite of steak and broccoli stir-fry. "I think he helped himself to Brooke's food."

Darcy took a bite of her chicken. "Tastes a lot like the place I get takeout. Glad I didn't have to be at home alone. I don't think I can handle that just yet."

"I'm glad I can be here with you. I have to work a long shift tomorrow," Jackson said. "I can see if one of the other K-9 officers has the day off." As a colleague, Darcy and her safety were important to the entire team.

"I'm hoping the lab will be open." She pulled her phone out. Harlan had left her a happy face emoticon. "Looks we're cleared to go back to work." A look of concern clouded Jackson's features. "I should be safe in the lab. I won't stay late or work alone."

"We can arrange for a police escort for you to and from work. At the very least, we'll have a patrol car go past your place and an officer go through the lab. Make sure there is no one suspicious hanging around."

A knot formed at the back of Darcy's neck. This was her reality; she had to accept it. It occurred to her that the officer she most wanted to escort her was sitting at the table with her. "Thanks for doing that. Maybe it will work out with the hours of your shift that you could escort me at least one way."

"I hope it works out that way, too. Smokey and I start at seven and get off at five."

The glow of affection she saw in Jackson's eyes made her heart flutter. "I can go early to the lab. We can just leave from here in the morning."

They finished their meal and cleaned up.

"I'm going to have to walk Brooke," Jackson said. "I'll leave Smokey here for protection and walk him separate."

"I know the drill. I'll lock the door behind you and not open it until I hear your knock."

"I'll knock five times. Three fast and two slow." He cupped his hand on her shoulder as he faced her. "That way you'll know it's me." He winked at her, which seemed to be his signature move and a way of telling her not to worry. "I'll press the entry code, but the knock will confirm that it's me. This woman is clever.

We shouldn't assume she wouldn't be able to figure out the entry code or know how to by-pass it."

Jackson called Brooke and hooked the leash on her. Darcy followed them out to the entry-way. Once the door closed behind Jackson, she locked it electronically.

She stepped away from the door and returned to the room with the puppies. Her stomach clenched as she collapsed into the rocking chair. She knew the fear would not go away until Jackson returned.

EIGHT

Jackson walked Brooke around the neighborhood. The person he'd seen in the hoodie leaning against the pole was no longer around. He circled the entire block, looking for anyone suspicious. There was a car parked at the curb with a woman sitting behind the wheel looking at her phone. She was wearing a hat, so he couldn't see her hair color. Nothing alarming about someone parked looking at their phone, but he couldn't take any chances. He made a mental note to come back this way to see if she was still around.

He and Brooke headed toward a pocket park. Though he was anxious to get back to Darcy, time with Brooke was always pleasant. She had potential as a K-9. It had taken some doing for the K-9 team to rescue her and the puppies, and the entire team was rallying for Brooke to become part of the unit. Her pups, too, upon time and assessment.

Brooke sniffed around some plants.

A man sitting on a bench, who was probably homeless, judging from his appearance, lifted his head and smiled when he saw Brooke.

"Hey, Rory. How you been girl?"

Brooke wagged her tail and pulled on the leash to get closer to the man, who reached out to pet her.

Jackson froze, feeling a tightening around his middle. "You know this dog?"

The man rubbed Brooke's head. "Sure, I seen this dog before. A while back, a tall guy with reddish hair kept trying to lure her out from where she was hiding. The dog got scared and ran away. He called her name over and over—Rory." The man leaned closer to the dog's head. "Good to see you again, girl."

A month ago, a man named Joel Carey had come into headquarters claiming that Brooke was named Rory and that the dog and pups were his. The man had seemed cagey and the team had brushed his claim off, gathering that he only wanted to sell Brooke and her pups. Brooke's rescue had been in the news. If Joel had been looking for Brooke, why hadn't there been posters put up? He hadn't come back, either, to demand the return of his dog, but maybe he was waiting for the unit to get back to him about the claim.

But now, seeing that Brooke was responsive to the name the man had used, caused Jackson to wonder if Joel, as unlikable as he was, had been telling the truth. Jackson walked back to the training center with a heavy heart. He didn't like the idea of having to give Brooke and her pups up.

The woman who had been sitting in her car looking at her phone was no longer around. A good sign, he supposed. He was still trying to process what the news that Brooke was Rory meant. He'd grown attached to the dog. He'd have to tell Gavin when he got on shift tomorrow. He turned the corner and knocked on the door of the training center.

He was glad to see Darcy's bright expression when she opened the door. He explained to her why he was upset.

"That would be a blow to the whole team if they had to turn Brooke and her brood over to that man," she said. "Especially Maverick. It sounds like this guy Joel is kind of a jerk."

They sat together and talked for a while longer before Jackson took Smokey out for his last walk of the night. The rest of the night was uneventful with each of them taking shifts to check on Maverick and to sleep. Gina had set up a cot in a back room since she was living full-time at the training center for the time being.

They arose early in the morning and cleaned up. Once Gina arrived, Jackson drove Darcy across Brooklyn to the lab. A lightness had come into her demeanor that he hadn't seen since the first attack at the lab. "I'm so glad to be getting back to work. I'm really far behind, and I have to do some prep for Reuben Bray's trial."

He pulled into the parking lot adjacent to the lab and pressed the brakes. "I'm sure it does feel good to get back to doing what you love." Already, Jackson felt a tight knot form in his stomach. He didn't want to leave her. "I'll wait until you are inside before I pull out of the lot."

She unclicked her seat belt and then looked at him. "Thank you, Jackson, for everything. I know it wasn't the best of circumstances, but last night, taking care of Maverick and everything… I enjoyed our time together."

"Me, too." He felt his cheeks heating up like he was some junior high kid and a girl had just told him she liked him. "I'll see you when I get off shift. If I get caught up with some investigation, just call headquarters. One of the K-9 team will be able to give you a ride home if I can't."

"Got it." She pushed open the door and hopped out of the SUV.

Warmth spread through his chest as he watched her cross the parking lot. Smokey made a yipping sound from the back seat. "I know she's all right, isn't she? She's a good friend."

Smokey whined.

Darcy swiped her card on sensor to open the door. She waved at Jackson before disappearing inside.

"Okay, maybe I think sometimes I would like for her to be more than a friend."

With Darcy still on his mind, Jackson shifted into Reverse. He wasn't even out of the parking lot when the first call came in for a cadaver dog.

He and Smokey stayed busy throughout the day. The second he had some downtime, he drove past the lab and Darcy's apartment building, checking for anything suspicious.

It wasn't until late in the afternoon that he was able to get back to headquarters. He entered the reception area, sending a smile to Penelope McGregor as he walked past the front desk. He was never able to pass Penny—or her brother, Detective Bradley McGregor—without thinking of the two cases the unit was working on. How hard it must be for the sib-lings to know their parents' killer had finally been identified but had eluded law enforcement, who were searching for him. He thought of Penny as a young child, her parents murdered while she was left unharmed—just like little Lucy Emery in the copycat murder several months ago. He knew there would be justice for both families. The team was getting closer to that every day.

As he stepped toward the offices, Noelle Orton, a rookie K-9 officer who used be a trainer, emerged looking distressed and holding an evidence bag filled with dog food. Her K-9 partner, Liberty, a yellow Lab with the distinctive black mark on her ear, walked beside her.

"Something wrong?" he asked, Smokey standing at attention beside him. He sure hoped not. For months now, an elusive drug smuggler they only knew as "Gunther" had put a bounty on Liberty's head because the K-9 was too good at her job and had foiled shipments in Atlantic Terminal. Attempts had made on Liberty's life, and Noelle kept her partner as safe as possible.

"I'm pretty sure someone tried to poison Liberty's food. Not sure how they got into the police vehicle. I keep some in there for when the shift gets long. Of course, she's smart enough not to eat it. She must have picked up on a scent on the food that wasn't mine or the poison has a distinct smell." Noelle lifted the bag. "I need to take this over to the lab to be tested."

"I can do that for you," Jackson said.

"This wouldn't have anything to do with a cute blond forensic scientist, would it? I hear the two of you have been spending lots of time together."

"We're just friends and, I'm sure you've heard, she needs some protection."

"I know. I feel awful about that. I was just teasing you." She smiled and handed him the bag.

Jackson looked at the bag of dog food. "This has to be connected to the bounty on Liberty's head from the gunrunner." Jackson had heard in the morning briefing that a raid had been set up on the gun smuggler's "office" in Coney Island today, but he hadn't heard the outcome. Gavin had previously made contact with an informant who'd given up Gunther's real name—Ivan Holland—and the location he was using on Coney Island.

"Anytime someone goes after Liberty, we have to assume Ivan is behind it. I'm sure the raid got him riled. Police showed up in riot gear. Ivan is still operating one step ahead of us—the place was empty." Noelle cast her gaze to the ground. "Unfortunately, the informant was swinging from the rafters."

It took a second for Jackson to process the gravity of what had taken place. A man trying to do the right thing had died. "I'm sorry to hear that." Jackson petted Liberty's head. "We'll catch him. We don't want anything happening to our girl, Liberty."

"Thanks, Jackson," Noelle said.

"Well, I'm headed over to the lab."

Jackson and Smokey left headquarters. As he drove the K-9 vehicle toward the forensics lab, he called Darcy, explaining that he had dog food sample she needed to test.

Darcy's voice came across the line sweet and clear. "A dog food sample, huh?"

"Yeah, someone may have tried to poison one of the K-9s," Jackson said. "Depending on traffic, I'm about twenty or so minutes from the lab."

"You don't have to text me when you get here. They installed an extra security measure. There is an outside camera and we have a monitor we can watch in the lab, so I'll see you pull into the parking lot and I'll come out and grab the bag from you. I love technology. I don't know why we didn't do it sooner."

Darcy sounded upbeat. She probably was feeling a lot better now that she was back at work.

"Got it. See you soon."

Traffic wasn't too congested and within twenty minutes, he pulled into the lot. He got out of his SUV and reached across the seat to grab the evidence bag. He stared through the windshield. Darcy stood with the door partially open, waiting for him.

An ultrasonic sound pummeled past his ear. It took only a nanosecond for him to register that it was likely a rifle shot aimed at Darcy. He crawled back into the vehicle and stayed low, noting that Darcy had shut the door and disappeared. He lifted his head up to peer though the back window. The shot had probably come from a tall building across the street. He stared back at the door of the lab. Had Darcy closed it in time, or had she been hit and was laying just inside?

The next shot pinged off his police vehicle. So, he was the target now. He was sure the shooter saw him as an obstacle in being able to get to Darcy. Not only was Jackson concerned that Darcy might have been hit, he was worried that a bullet would find Smokey, who was confined in his crate.

After calling for backup, Jackson slipped out of his vehicle. He crouched, using the door screen for just a second. A moment later, Darcy saw Jackson and Smokey in hot pursuit.

Two patrol cars pulled into the lot and uniformed officers got out. She could not see Jackson or the woman anymore.

The two officers ran off-screen in the same direction Jackson had gone.

Darcy heard gunshots. She closed her eyes and said a prayer for their safety.

She stared at the screen, which only showed the parking lot and the unoccupied police cars. The sound of her breathing seemed to intensify as she waited.

"Hope they're okay," Harlan said. He patted her shoulder, but she picked up on the fear in his voice.

The moment seemed to last forever before the two officers ran back on-screen. She let out a heavy sigh. "They're okay." The officers returned to their patrol cars and sped out of the lot.

Jackson and Smokey finally came on-screen, running toward the building. "Jackson is coming to the lab. I'll go let him in."

After unlocking the door to the lab, she ran down the hallway and held open the main door. Jackson and Smokey stood outside and she resisted the urge to fall into his arms. She was so

as a shield. Maybe he could get to the shooter before she got away—assuming it was the woman who had been after Darcy, which was his best guess.

He studied the windows of the building across the street, not seeing any movement. The shooter may have taken the shots and run, realizing that she would be caught if she stayed around.

His phone rang. It was Darcy.

He breathed a sigh of relief. "Are you okay?"

"Yes, got back inside in time and ran back to the lab. The bullet is probably stuck the door. I think I might be able to extract it later. I saw on the monitor that she's taking shots at you now."

Jackson glanced across the street. No one entered or exited the building but that didn't mean there wasn't a back way out. "I'm just in the way. I'm sure she doesn't like that I can protect you. She's trying to get at you and figures part of that is taking me out of the equation."

"You're a sitting duck out there. I don't want you to be hurt."

"Darcy, I have a job to do. Backup is on the way," he said. "You stay inside where it's safe. I'm going to see if we can catch her and end this thing." He hung up before she could protest. Smokey would be less of an easy target if he wasn't secured in the crate. Jackson knew he didn't have time to wait for backup if he was going to get this woman. He and Smokey had to act now.

Darcy watched on the monitor as Jackson unloaded Smokey and then drew his weapon. He couched low, using the cars as cover as he moved toward the street and the building opposite. Her lungs felt like an elephant was sitting on them. "Why doesn't he wait for the other cops?"

"He probably figures he doesn't have that kind of time." Harlan stood beside her, staring at the monitor, as well. "He'll be all right, Darcy. He's a good cop with a great partner."

Her gaze shot upward as she heard the pounding of footsteps above her. There were occupied offices up there, but the noise was always at a minimum. Could the shooter have snuck out the back of the building and made her way across the street?

The last time she was attacked in the lab, the perp had crawled through the ductwork to get to this floor. "Maybe we should lock the door to the lab too not just the outside door." She hurried across the floor and pressed in the code that would lock the door. When she checked the monitor, Jackson had made it across the street, but had made an about-face

with Smokey and was headed back toward the lab. He'd seen something on this side of the street.

Harlan closed his laptop.

More footsteps echoed above them. Then the world fell silent.

A moment later, the door to the lab rattled. Someone was trying to get in.

Whoever was shaking the door stopped. Several more tense seconds passed. Darcy stood paralyzed as a rifle shot blasted a hole through the door. Followed immediately by another. Darcy jumped back. The shooter was going to blast her way in.

Both Darcy and Harlan dropped to the floor and crawled toward the far side of the lab, seeking cover behind a desk. There was only one way in and out of the lab. Darcy braced for another rifle shot, but then heard retreating footsteps. Something had scared the shooter off. The hallway where the shooter had been had a window that looked out onto the parking lot. Maybe she'd seen Jackson headed back this way.

"There, in the parking lot." Harlan peered around the desk and pointed at the monitor.

Darcy ran over to it just in time to see a person, probably a woman, running. She had a rifle slung over her shoulder. She was on-

relieved neither he nor Smokey had been hurt. "I'm so glad you're okay."

"Suspect got away. She had a car with a driver waiting. Patrol cars are going to try to catch her." Jackson glanced around nervously. "I don't think it's good for me to stand outside like this—now that she's decided to come after me. A drive-by is still a possibility."

She stepped to one side. "Oh, sorry."

Jackson and Smokey came inside, allowing the door to lock behind him. "And it wasn't good for you to be out in the open like that, either." He reached up, brushing his hand over her cheek with a feather-light touch. "You should not have stood in the doorway like that."

"I know. I have to keep reminding myself," Darcy said. His touch, though brief, had made her heart beat faster for a whole different reason. "I was scared for you and Smokey. I heard the gunshots and I thought maybe one of you had been hit. When I saw you were okay, I just wasn't thinking for a moment."

"You don't need to worry about me. Being in danger is just the nature of my work, Darcy. Good thing you don't date cops."

"That doesn't matter," she said. "Even as a friend, I was worried for you." Her hand brushed his sleeve.

"I appreciate that." He looked down at her and, for a moment, a charge of electricity seemed to pass between them. The thought zinged through her mind that if Jackson wasn't a police officer, she could so fall for him.

She took a step back. "So that woman must have been shooting from across the street and then snuck over her to try to get at me."

"It looks that way," Jackson said. "Another lab is going to have to come in and process all this. I'd say you and Harlan are done working for the day."

Darcy clenched her jaw. More delays in getting her work done. "You can at least bring me that dog food sample, and I will catalog it. Hopefully processing this scene won't take long and I can get back to work."

After commanding Smokey to stay, Jackson swung the door open and disappeared outside. Darcy stepped out of view as the door eased shut. She could see the holes in the metal doors where the bullets had gone through. Though the chances of the shooter coming back were slim, she knew she needed to make a habit of being hypervigilant. She kneeled down to pet Smokey. The dog licked her face as if to comfort her. He must have picked up on her agitation. She was still stirred up from having been shot at through the locked door.

Jackson knocked on the outside door. She rose and pushed it open, careful not to stand in the open doorway. He handed her the dog food sample. "When you do get a chance to process it, you can phone headquarters to let Noelle and Gavin know."

"We're so backed up," Darcy said. "I wish I could get my work done."

The evidence for the Emery case had been put on the back burner for now. Thankfully, it hadn't been destroyed in the previous attack. Once she isolated the DNA, Darcy; hoped she would at least be able to rule out one suspect. Randall Gage, who was still at large, was a DNA match for the double homicide twenty years ago that was so close to home for the K-9 Unit. Gage had murdered Eddie and Anna McGregor, the parents of Bradley and Penelope McGregor. Either Randall had committed the Emery murder, too, or they were looking at a copycat. She knew the unit was thinking copycat, which meant there was another killer out there—and this time, they didn't know his identity.

"You and Harlan should probably go home. I can drive you. I'll talk to Gavin to see if we can have a patrol car put outside your place."

The last thing she wanted to do was to sit at home like some kind of a prisoner. "Look,

I did have time to put together a list of potential females who might have a grudge against me. Can you go with me to question them?" At least that way she would be doing something to end this nightmare.

"Sure," he said. "If I can clear it with Gavin."

Once they had access to the lab again, the next thing on her list to process was the gun found close to where Griffin Martel had been killed. Maybe she could at least make some headway on that case.

NINE

By the time Jackson had gotten the okay from
Gavin to start working through Darcy's list
of suspects, the parking lot and the lab were
swarming with law enforcement and forensic
staff from the Manhattan unit.

Darcy and Jackson waited in the hallway
while the techs moved in and out, processing
both the outside door and the door that led to
the lab. They had also gone across the street
to see if they could find where the shooter had
lain in wait.

Harlan had already left.

It was unlikely that the woman would come
back, but Jackson knew he had to heed his
own advice and exercise caution at all times.
He looked at Darcy. "You ready to go?" He'd
snagged an extra bulletproof vest for her given
they were going to be out in the open questioning suspects. He and Smokey already had
theirs on.

She nodded and they stepped outside.

Jackson took up a position on one side of Darcy and Smokey walked on the other as they approached his vehicle. He did a visual of the area and across the street once Darcy was safely inside the SUV.

Jackson loaded Smokey back up and got in behind the wheel. "Who's our first suspect?"

"A woman named Lydia Harmon. My work helped put her brother away for robbery. She claimed her brother was innocent. She sent several threatening emails after the trial. She's ex-military. I know that this woman who is after me hires goons, but she's the one doing the shooting at me and now at you. Lydia probably has some marksman skills because of her background."

"Sounds like a smart place to start," Jackson said. "Are you hungry? We can grab a quick bite somewhere first."

"Starved," she said.

"The safest place would be where cops hang out. I know a good diner near a police precinct nearby. They have a little of everything. And always a lot of cops at the counter and tables."

"Sounds good to me," Darcy said.

"We can get it to go, so we're not inside long."

Jackson drove through downtown Brooklyn. He waited for a spot by the diner to open up and pulled in. They got out of the SUV together.

The noise of people chatting and eating greeted them when Jackson opened the door. The air smelled of grease and salt.

Jackson pointed up at a whiteboard. "Any of the specials look good to you? They bring those out real fast."

They took seats at the counter. Though this was probably the safest place for him to take Darcy if she had to be out in the open, Jackson's nerves were still on edge.

"The fried chicken special sounds great to me," she said.

"Same here. You can put in the order. I'm going to watch the room." He swung around on his stool.

Fear flashed through her eyes and then she turned to get the waiter's attention. Jackson studied the people at the tables, giving a nod toward the officers he recognized from working across Brooklyn. He was aware that even the off-duty officers were probably armed. He felt himself relax a little. Only a fool would try something in a place that was so packed with cops.

Once they had their food, they walked back to the SUV and got inside, the delicious smell of their takeout making his stomach growl.

Darcy opened her to-go box and took a bite of her chicken. "This is really good."

He smiled. "Another fine dining experience brought to you by Jackson and Smokey."

"No. I mean it, this is really tasty," she said.

He found himself wishing that he could take her out to a nice restaurant. What a difference from a few days ago when he'd taken her to the pizza joint so she wouldn't think they were on a date. As much as he had dug his heels in, he had to admit his heart was opening up to the possibility of something more than friendship with her. Too bad she didn't date cops.

"Why are you looking at me like that?" Darcy munched on a French fry.

He shook his head. "Nothing. Just thinking." He had no idea if her feelings had shifted. He kind of doubted it. A woman who draws a line in the sand about not dating cops probably wouldn't change her mind.

"Darcy, that rule that you have about not dating cops, is there a reason behind it?"

Darcy took a nibble on her French fry and chewed for a moment. "If I let the personal get mixed up with the professional, it can cause trouble for cases. In my job, integrity is everything, and it can be the difference between a guilty man going to jail or walking." An intensity he hadn't heard from her before colored her words. "I just figured if I couldn't separate my romantic feelings for someone from my work, the safest thing to do was to not ever let the personal and professional get tangled together."

That settled that. He sat staring out of the window for a moment, not sure what to say. "I get it." He turned the key in the ignition. "Where are we going to talk to Lydia Harmon?"

Darcy crushed the cardboard container her meal had been in. "She's works security at the Brooklyn Navy Yard. She's on duty now. I got the information from her roommate by pretending to be an old friend. She doesn't know we're going to interview her. I think the element of surprise comes in handy when you're trying to get the truth out of someone."

"You managed to do that?" He continued to be impressed at how smart and clever Darcy was. "You may have missed your calling as a detective."

She smiled. "No, my calling is as a forensics expert. I'm sure of it. But thanks for the compliment."

He shifted into Reverse. "Let's go check it out."

As they drew closer to the Brooklyn Navy Yard, they had a view of lower Manhattan across the water. Though the over two hundred acres of buildings, cranes and dry docks was still called the "Navy Yard," it hadn't been used for building and repairing ships for years. It had been turned into an industrial park. A museum, businesses and eateries now occupied the multiple buildings on the site.

Darcy checked her phone again. "The security office is in Building 77, first floor. If Lydia's not there, they will know where to find her."

Jackson wondered if it would be best for Darcy to stay in the SUV with Smokey with the doors locked.

His thoughts must have been evident in his expression. "I'm going with you," she said. "The last time I stayed in a locked car, it didn't make a bit of difference in keeping me safe."

Jackson opened his mouth to protest.

"If we have learned anything, it's that I'm in danger no matter what," she said. "Besides, I'm the one with the detective skills, remember."

Jackson shook his head and chuckled. "Okay. Stay close to Smokey and me."

As they walked up Flushing Avenue toward Vanderbilt, Jackson went on high alert. He paid attention to the people around him, but the thing that concerned him the most were the location possibilities that someone might take up a position to fire a rifle. There was no way the suspect could know ahead of time that Jackson and Darcy were going here, but they might have been followed.

He had to assume that they were still on the attacker's radar. History had proven that anytime he let his guard down, bad things happened. Though it would take a moment for someone with a rifle to get into position, there were numerous possibilities in the multistoried buildings around them, some of which were only partially occupied. If the female attacker had a goon helping her out, there was no telling what could happen.

Once they were inside Building 77, Jackson relaxed a little. They were most vulnerable out on the street. A placard inside the lobby showed that there were plenty of businesses inside the building. They walked across the lobby to the security office. The woman behind the desk informed them that Lydia was probably at the museum.

A knot of tension formed at the back of Jackson's neck. That meant going back outside on the street. Once they were outside, Jackson stayed close to Darcy while Darcy held Smokey's leash so he could walk on the other side of her.

"Pay attention to Smokey," Jackson advised. "He's a good barometer for threats and danger.

His hackles will go up, or he'll stutter or stop in his step. He might lift his nose."

He allowed Darcy and Smokey to enter the museum first so he could give the street one final survey. People bustled by without glancing in his direction.

The entrance to the museum had a huge metal anchor the size of a whale. A docent stood by it, explaining to a small cluster of people how much it weighed.

Darcy pointed across the room. "There, I just saw a woman in uniform disappear around that corner. That's probably Lydia."

They hurried across the crowded floor, pressing through a group of people. Darcy glanced over her shoulder and then Smokey stopped.

Jackson pressed closer to her, touching her arm just above the elbow. "What?"

She shook her head. "Just a feeling."

Whatever had caused Darcy to slow down had also set off an alarm bell for Smokey.

The woman in uniform returned to the open area.

"That's Lydia Harmon," Darcy said.

The security guard made eye contact with them and stepped in their direction.

Smoky jerked on the leash and faced the

entrance to the building. He emitted a sharp, intense bark. Darcy whirled around, as well.

Her voice slipped into monotone and grew as cold as ice. "It's her. She's here."

Jackson stared at the crowd, not seeing anyone that resembled the woman he only gotten a glimpse of at the lab. "Are you sure?"

Lydia Harmon had stepped close enough to talk to them. "You look like you need something. Can I help you folks?"

The crowd cleared. A woman dressed in running clothes, a jacket and a baseball hat, locked in to Jackson's gaze for less than a second before whirling around and leaving the museum. She wasn't running, but she was walking at a brisk pace so as not to call attention to herself.

It was the expression—that intense look of fear on her face—that tipped Jackson off. That had to be her. Jackson sprinted across the museum floor.

He hurried outside, scanning the sidewalk filled with people, not seeing the woman. The baseball hat had been an indistinct color.

The crowds cleared on part of the sidewalk. He saw a pale baseball hat tossed on the path that led to the shipyard. She'd been smart enough to toss the one thing that might allow him to pick her out of a crowd. But dumb enough to leave something behind that a forensic scientist could test for DNA to ID her. He wished he had Smokey with him; even though the K-9 was trained to find human remains, not track suspects on the run, Smokey had helped with the watcher in the park.

After pulling the evidence bag from the cargo pocket of his uniform, Jackson bagged the hat, scanned the faces on the street, and kept walking at a brisk pace. Most likely the suspect would try to blend in with the rest of the crowd.

He keyed his radio and requested backup while he sped up his pace. He gave a description of the woman to Dispatch. "We need to cover as many streets as possible. I don't want her getting away."

"Ten-Four," said the dispatcher. "Looks like three units are in the area. We can't cover all the streets leading into the Navy Yard, but they can run a patrol for several blocks each. They should be in place in less than ten minutes."

Ten minutes was a long time where a search was concerned. And if she had parked close by, she would be able to get to her car and escape.

Still watching the sidewalks filled with people, he backtracked to get his K-9, noting that Darcy and Smokey had emerged from the museum. Smokey might be able to pick up on a scent while they waited for the tracking dogs to arrive.

Before he could get back to Darcy, Smokey jerked on the leash and took off running along the street, dragging Darcy with him. The dog had noticed or smelled something.

Jackson sprinted to catch up with them. He couldn't leave Darcy exposed. There was a chance the woman would turn on her and take her.

Or worse, if she was armed with a handgun, she might be able to shoot Darcy and disappear into the crowd.

Darcy ran hard to keep up with Smokey. The K-9 must have seen or smelled something. He seemed intent on crossing the street. She trusted the dog's training over anything her senses might tell her. The woman at the entrance to the museum had acted very suspiciously. Though Darcy had never gotten a clear look at the woman's face, there was something about the way she'd moved that was distinct. She ran like an athlete.

Darcy picked up her pace. Off to the side, she saw Jackson coming toward her.

He caught up with her just as Smokey stopped outside a shop that sold imported home goods. The dog paced back and forth.

"Do you think she went in there?"

"It's worth a shot." Jackson reached for Smokey's leash.

They stepped inside. The place was more like a warehouse than a shop, with its high ceilings, and shelving and displays that were almost as high.

"There is no safe place for you right now," Jackson said, "so just stay close to me and Smokey."

"Two sets of eyes are better than one," she said.

"Actually, we have three sets of eyes and one good nose."

They worked their way up one aisle and down another. The final aisle was much more crowded. Darcy pressed close to Jackson as they squeezed through the shoppers. A woman bumped shoulders with Darcy, setting off her personal alarm bells.

"Oh, sorry," she said.

Darcy looked at the woman. Not their suspect. "No problem."

Smokey jerked on the leash, indicating the entrance to the shop. "Let's get back outside," Jackson said.

As they stepped out onto the sidewalk, Jackson's radio blared. Something about units being in place.

A popping sound reverberated in Darcy's ear, followed quickly by another gunshot. Jackson pushed her to the wall, dropping Smokey's leash. The dog paced and barked but remained close.

The crowd dispersed, running in all directions.

Jackson pressed his face very close to Darcy's. "She's shooting at us from the second floor. Probably with a handgun. She didn't have a rifle with her, and no way could she have had time to stash it. She must have followed us here. But how could she have made it across the street and upstairs to shoot at us as we were leaving? That makes no sense." He shook his head. "Get back in the shop. You'll be safe where there are lots of people. Take Smokey, just to be sure."

Jackson took off before she could respond. He spoke frantically into his radio.

Darcy flattened against the wall and worked her way toward the shop entrance. There was no one else on the sidewalk. She slipped into the shop, which was still crowded, though everyone had moved toward the rear of the shop. Some people were talking on their phones in urgent voices. Others were just pressed against the wall, staring at nothing. No one was shopping. She stood off to the side at the back of the store, as well, separated from the cluster of people.

Her heart squeezed tight with fear for Jackson's safety. Smokey sat at her feet, moving his head back and forth, watching the other people.

Something hard pressed against her back and a male voice spoke into her ear. "Drop the dog leash and come with me. You make a fuss and I'll shoot you and the dog on the spot. You understand?"

Darcy shook her head. When she dropped the leash, Smokey turned to face her. His face filled with expectation, awaiting a command.

"Tell him to stay," the man whispered in her ear.

"Sit. Stay, Smokey." Her voice quivered with fear.

The dog did as he was told.

"Now let's you and me head out the back door."

Darcy glanced around at the crowd, wondering if she could get someone's attention before a bullet entered her back. Not likely, as the man sounded serious. Would he risk being caught? The ideal plan was probably to take her someplace more secluded. Either way, it was clear his intent was to kill her.

TEN

Jackson hurried up the stairs. He was greeted by a long hallway with doors indicating various offices, lawyers and accountants mostly. He could only guess at where the shots had come from. Judging from the sound, they had not been from a rifle but a handgun. He wondered if the woman intended to get them into a vulnerable place and then take her shot at Darcy. A handgun didn't have the long-distant accuracy of a rifle, so chances were she'd been firing from the second floor. But still, how had she so quickly gotten from the shop to here and in place to shoot at them?

There were three possibilities for where the shots had originated. The first door indicated the office of a financial planner. Jackson knocked on the door.

"Yes, come in." The voice sounded frightened.

Jackson opened the door and stuck his head

in. The first thing he saw was a desk with two computer monitors and a headset that had been tossed on the floor. A man in a suit was pressed against a far wall. He looked at Jackson's uniform. The man's stiff shoulders relaxed a little. "I heard the shots. What's going on?"

Off to his side, Jackson heard banging and shuffling. He poked his head out of the office just in time to see a woman running toward the stairwell.

Jackson sprinted after her. By the time he flung the door open and glanced up the twisting stairwell, the woman was not in sight, though he heard the tap, tap, tap of footsteps above him. She had to be in good shape to have run that quickly, but why not run down to the street?

Jackson raced up the stairs until he reached the rooftop where there was a garden and several storage sheds. No one was currently working in the garden. He scanned side to side. The rooftops were connected well enough that you could run from one to the other. There was a small group of people several rooftops over. They were sitting at tables and had a barbecue going. He didn't see the woman anywhere. That meant she must be hiding behind or in one of the storage sheds.

Pulling his weapon, he checked around the first storage shed. When he tried to open it, he found it was locked. He moved to the second shed, making a sweeping pattern with his gun. He moved toward the next shed.

A bullet whizzed by him, so close that his skin tingled and his eardrum felt like it been hit with a tiny hammer. He fell to the ground and then peered up. The shot had come from the garden of corn and sunflowers, which were high and thick enough to hide someone. The foliage rustled and a woman half rose then took off in the direction of the next rooftop. Would she risk trying to jump across? She sought shelter behind the final shed just as Jackson rose and aimed his weapon. He didn't want to kill her, only wound her.

"Police!" he said. "Come out with your hands up!"

He stepped steadily toward the shed. In the distance, he heard sirens. Once the shooting had happened, NYPD sent all kinds of backup, not just the units that were in the area. Judging from the sound of the sirens, some were probably still five minutes away.

"Give yourself up," he said. "This place is going to be surrounded in just minutes." He kept his weapon aimed at the shed as he moved in.

A strange noise not too far from the shed

caught his attention. It sort of sounded like metal creaking or something that needed to be greased. Still on high alert, he raced to the edge of the building. Using the shed to shield her from view, the woman had climbed down a fire escape as far as it would take her. She was now hanging from a windowsill. He watched as she dropped the ten feet to the ground and raced up a back alley. She ran like lightning. No way could he make that climb and catch up with her.

He clicked on his radio. "Suspect is on the run. Looks like she's headed up an alley toward Flushing. Suspect is considered armed and dangerous."

He hurried back to the stairwell and sprinted down, taking the stairs two at a time. Though he headed up the alley, running as fast as he could, he knew that his efforts were probably futile. The woman had some athletic chops; he had to hand it to her.

He ran all the way out to Flushing Avenue, searching everywhere while he caught his breath. The crowds were just too abundant. It would be too easy for her to blend in. The rest of the NYPD would put an all points out for her, and the search would continue in a five-block radius around the Navy Yard.

He pulled out the bagged hat he'd picked up.

One of the tracker dogs might be able to find her. He hurried back to the building where he'd left Darcy and Smokey. Outside the building, Tyler Walker was waiting with Dusty, along with dozens of other police units, both K-9 and patrol. Tyler must have been one of the units that was close by to get here so fast.

Jackson handed Tyler the hat. Dusty picked up on a scent right away. After Jackson briefed the other officers on all that happened, he headed into the imported home goods store. At least Darcy had been kept safe.

He hurried inside. Most of the people were still gathered at the back of the store. Their expressions communicated fear and alarm.

He moved up one aisle and down the other, not seeing Darcy or Smokey. He stepped into the third aisle. When Smokey came running toward him, dragging the leash, Jackson knew something was terribly wrong.

Still pressing the gun in her back, the man led her onto a back street. At least ten people stood in the street, which was normally not that busy as it was the backside of businesses where the Dumpsters were kept.

He spoke through gritted teeth. "Where are all these people coming from?"

She'd heard the sirens. NYPD had probably

sent many units to deal with the active shooter. These people probably had taken shelter in the back alleys thinking it was safer from potential violence.

"Once your friend shot at me, I'm sure the NYPD pulled out all the stops."

"Shut up," he said. "Do what I say." He poked her with the barrel of the gun. His free hand was wrapped around her forearm. To the world, they probably looked like a couple out for a stroll. Though Darcy thought the expression on her face might indicate they were a couple who had just had a fight.

She scanned the faces around her. No one was even looking in their direction.

Yelling for help or that she was being kidnapped might mean he would just shoot her on the spot and run, aiming the gun at anyone who tried to take him down. The police were close by…if she could just get on a street where they were. If Jackson had figured out what happened to her, he might have given the other officers a description of her.

"This place is crawling with police." She still felt the pressure of the gun against her back. "Even if you shoot me, you won't get away."

"I'm Brooklyn born and raised. I know every

back alley and shortcut." The man sounded nervous to her.

He pushed her forward around a corner and onto another street. Two blocks up, she saw the flashing lights of a police vehicle. He yanked her back around the corner. He must have seen it, too.

"Like I said. You're surrounded. Why don't you let me go? You can get away."

He pushed on her back. "Let's just keep going down this street."

Darcy walked, moving her eyes while her head remained still. She had to find the opportunity for escape. "You're not even doing this for yourself, are you? It's that woman who is behind it all." Maybe she could get some information out of him. Maybe she could break his resolve. "What is she to you, your girlfriend?"

"Shut up, I said." His voice broke. "I should just shoot you now. Take my chances."

Of course, if she ended up dead, any information Darcy gathered would not help anyone. She could tell the man was growing more frustrated. He could be pushed toward giving up as fast as he could be pushed toward just shooting her.

They walked by a building where Darcy noticed a homeless man was passed out. He wouldn't have slept through all the sirens. He must been unconscious from some kind of drug or too much alcohol. The shooter stopped and stared at the prone man. "It would be nothing to shoot you and leave you to look like you were sleeping just like him."

Fear charged through her like a raging bull. There would be no time to scream even at this close range. "There would be blood. People would see."

Still gripping her upper arm, he pushed the gun barrel into her back again. "Up there, that street."

The street he was pointing to looked like more of an alley or side street. Chances were, it would be deserted. She had to get away before they turned the corner.

Sirens sounded in the distance, but some were growing louder, maybe two blocks away. The man hesitated in his step. His grip on her arm loosened. This was her opportunity.

She wrenched her body, wrestling free of his grip. His gun was visible. She shouted, "Help! Help me!"

Several people looked in her direction.

The man pointed his gun at them. "You come at me and I'll shoot."

The few people who had looked her way took a step back, fear clouding their expressions just as a patrol car rounded the corner.

The man shoved her forward and ran down the alley just as the patrol officer got out of his car.

Darcy fell, putting her hands out in front of her to brace for impact with the concrete. The patrol officer assessed the situation. One of the onlookers pointed up the alley. The officer sprinted toward the street where the armed man had gone.

An older woman came up to Darcy and held out her hand to her. Darcy could barely stand. She felt like every bone in her body was vibrating. She'd managed to stay levelheaded through the whole ordeal. Now that she was safe, all the fear and panic she'd held at bay flooded through her like a tsunami.

The older woman didn't say anything, only patted her shoulder. The rest of the people watched Darcy as she brushed off her pant legs. Her heart was still racing.

Jackson and Smokey came around the corner. She stumbled toward them and fell into his arms.

He held her and whispered in her ear. "It's all right now. You're safe." He drew her closer. "I was so worried about you, Darcy."

"He could have killed me." The realization made her weak-kneed all over again. But it was different now with Jackson so close. As she reveled in the safety she felt in Jackson's arms, a sense of calm returned.

Smokey whined at his feet. He wagged his tail when Darcy lifted her head to look in his direction. "You were worried, too, weren't you?"

Jackson tightened his embrace and drew her closer. She had the sense that he wanted the moment to last as much as she did.

He pulled free of the hug and looked into her eyes. "Let's get you home. There are plenty of officers here to continue searching," he said. "You have been through enough for one day. I think my priority needs to be with getting you home safe."

She so appreciated his sensitivity to how shredded she felt right now. They waited around for a while longer. After giving their statements, they returned to his SUV and loaded up.

He talked as they drove through traffic. "Considering everything that has happened, I think I can get a patrol car to park outside your house for the whole night."

"That would be great." She was still trying to calm down. Part of her wished that it would be Jackson parked outside her place. She only truly felt safe when she was with him.

He made the call to Gavin while they were en route. Jackson explained the situation and added, "She needs a higher level of security than I alone can manage in my off-duty hours." He glanced over at her and gave her his trademark wink.

"Let me put you on hold one minute," Gavin said. "I'll see what I can authorize."

Jackson turned to Darcy. "I'm sure they will put someone in place. If not, I'll park outside your building."

His offer touched her heart. "But you have to go on shift in the morning. You'd be exhausted."

"I'd do it for you, Darcy."

Jackson had the phone on speaker and Gavin's voice came back across the line. "We can have a car outside her building within half an hour."

"Ten-Four," Jackson responded.

They fell into a comfortable silence. It was still early in the evening, the sky had just started to turn gray.

Though her heartbeat had returned to normal, Darcy was stirred up from the trauma of having had a gun held on her again. She thanked God that she was alive. That she had such a good friend like Jackson. And then she tried to focus on something positive. "It will be good to see my sister and my cat again."

Jackson found a parking space a few blocks

from her building. "I'll walk you to your door and then I'm going to stay parked outside until a patrol car shows up."

"You can come inside, if you like."

"Your sister's been home for most of the day, right?"

"Yes," she said. "So what you're saying is that there is no chance of anyone waiting to jump me inside." She was a little disappointed to not be able to spend even a few more minutes in Jackson's company.

Leaving Smokey in the car, they made their way up the sidewalk. "I'll watch the street, and I'll text you when the patrol unit shows. He or she will stay here all night until I can come to get you in the morning."

They stood outside her apartment building door, facing each other. "Thank you for everything, Jackson."

A moment passed as they gazed at each other.

Darcy fell into his arms again, seeking the comfort of his strength and steady nature. She pulled back and looked into his eyes. "Could you call me instead of texting when the patrol officer shows up? I'd love to hear the sound of your voice. I don't know… It gives me a sense of peace."

"Sure." He seemed amused by her request. "You have a good rest of your night."

"Okay." She fumbled in her purse for the key, grateful that there was a streetlamp to illuminate the entranceway so she could see to shove it into the lock.

Opening the door, she turned back to look at Jackson. "See you in the morning."

"Remember not to stand in front of the windows," he said.

"I know," she said.

"Sorry to sound like a broken record. I just want to make sure I see your smiling face and dimples in the morning."

His remark softened the blow of having to live with the reality of her life being under constant threat. They both seemed to be prolonging the goodbye. Jackson's company and protection felt so natural, like breathing. Darcy found herself not wanting to be away from him.

She stepped inside, closing the door behind her, then headed to her apartment.

Her sister was sitting at the table working on a laptop. She smiled up at her. Mr. Tubbs rested on the couch. This was home.

Darcy collapsed on the couch and petted the cat. "I've had quite the day."

She stared at the ceiling thinking about her growing attachment to Jackson and how hopeless she felt about it.

ELEVEN

The next morning, Jackson got a call from Darcy saying she was free to go back to work, so he picked her up. After dropping her at the lab, he found himself distracted at the morning briefing for the Brooklyn K-9 Unit. His mind was on Darcy and her safety. And if he was honest with himself, he would rather be with her than anywhere else, not just to protect her but because he genuinely liked being around her.

From the front of the room, Gavin briefed them on what had happened to Darcy yesterday, advising that any unit that was in the area of the lab or her home should be on the lookout for anything suspicious and report it in right away.

"We have the man in custody who held her at gunpoint. He's not talking. We believe he is just hired muscle and a woman is behind the attacks on Darcy Fields. Now, Detective

Walker will brief us on the Emery double homicide and the progress made in locating the person little Lucy had said she missed during a recent interview." *I miss Andy* was all Lucy had said on the subject, and her aunt and uncle had confirmed that there was no one named Andy in her life. "We believe," Gavin continued, "that finding this person of interest might help us make a break in the murder of her parents. Tyler?"

Tyler rose from his chair and walked to the front of the room. He had told Jackson that he felt like the Emery case was deeply personal, not just because Lucy's aunt had married one of their own—Detective Nate Slater—but because every time he looked at Lucy, he thought about his own eighteen-month-old little girl who was also growing up without her mother. But they were both grateful that Lucy had a loving mother figure in her aunt and that Willow and Nate were in the process of adopting her.

Tyler ran his hand, through his blond hair and cleared his throat. "As you know, several times I have been out to where the Emerys lived, trying to track down this 'Andy' that Lucy refers to. We've found several people who go by that name or a similar-sounding name, but when we show Lucy a photograph, she shakes her head."

Jackson picked up on the frustration in Tyler's voice.

"What about a kid who goes by that name? Maybe from the playground or day care in that neighborhood," suggested Jackson.

"Covered those bases," Tyler said. "Also looked into the possibility that it was a senior citizen she might have had contact within the neighborhood." Tyler shook his head. "I feel like I'm at a dead end."

Detective Nate Slater spoke up. "We really need a break in this case for Lucy's sake. I need to know my little girl is safe." His voice filled with intense emotion.

Jackson clenched his teeth. When was this case going to break? "I agree. This thing needs to move forward. If we can't track down this Andy guy, maybe Darcy can get something usable off the fiber from the crime scene."

Gavin thanked Tyler and excused everyone from the briefing, reminding them to stay safe. Officers with K-9 partners dispersed in different directions. Jackson was walking past the front desk counter, where Penny MacGregor typed on a computer keyboard, when his phone rang. He recognized the number as Darcy's.

He pressed the connect button. "Darcy, how are you?"

"So, I thought you might want to know that the gun you found in the trash can in Prospect Park is a ballistics match for the one that killed Griffin Martel."

"That's good news, right? It's a step forward in that case." He'd detected a slight lilt in Darcy's voice that he had not heard before.

"That's not what has me bent out of shape, though. I also got a print match off the gun." She hesitated for a moment. It sounded like she had taken in a sharp, quick breath. "You're not going to believe who it belongs to."

Even through the phone, he detected a level of tension. "Try me?"

"Reuben Bray."

It took Jackson a moment to process what she'd said. When the information sunk in, it was like a slap across his jaw. "You mean the guy who is sitting in jail right now and has been for months?"

"The press is going to have a field day with this," Darcy said. "But I can't avoid it. I have to hold a press conference. They already think I didn't do my job with Reuben's case." Her voice filled with tension. "I can't prove it, but my gut tells me the evidence was planted to make me look bad. Griffin Martel's death somehow connects back to Reuben Bray—and not because Reuben killed him. That would be impossible. Someone is trying to set me up to look incompetent. It's the only thing that makes sense."

"The trial is soon, right? There's a potential that the whole thing could be thrown out because of this," Jackson noted.

"Exactly, maybe someone is trying to bungle the trial so Reuben walks," she said. "The one bit of forensic evidence that supports my theory is that the fingerprints were a match, but they were partials. There was some smudging and smearing, which makes me think that someone wearing gloves could have fired the gun after Reuben held it."

"Is that something that could be brought up in court for Griffin Martel's case?"

"It's a stretch. We really need more to go on," she said. "Plus, it's not the Griffin Martel case I'm worried about. It's Reuben Bray's that this taints."

"When is your press conference?"

"Toward the end of my day. We've already sent out notice to the news outlets. We're holding it inside the lab so there is no chance of that woman shooting at me from far away. There's a small conference room at the end of the hallway."

Although he was sure security measures were in place, the press conference meant lots of strange people milling around the lab. A fake press pass could be used easily enough if it wasn't examined closely. Darcy would still be in danger. "I'll still be on shift, but I'm sure Gavin will let me be there for protection as long as Smokey and I are not out on a call."

"That makes me feel a little better," she said. "This is going to be a long day."

"If you are feeling up to it… Maybe when you're done with the reporters, we can go out to Rikers and talk to Reuben. He could have set this whole thing up from his jail cell."

"Oh, I'm more than feeling up to it. I want this resolved. There is no way I will let Reuben Bray walk out of that jail a free man. See you later today."

"If I can't be there for the press conference, I'll make sure someone from the unit is, Darcy. We have your back."

"You have no idea how good it is to hear that."

He clicked off the phone. Stirred up by the news that Darcy had given him, he and Smokey headed out to the patrol SUV. He made the decision that when he went over to provide protection for Darcy, he would try to commandeer the help of at least one other K-9 officer.

* * *

Darcy's stomach did flip-flops as she watched the security screen in the lab that provided a view of the parking lot. Several press vans had already pulled in. "They're early."

Harlan cupped a hand on her shoulder. "I'll point them toward the conference room. You don't have to make an appearance until your protection shows up."

"Thanks, Harlan."

Harlan stepped toward the door. "Lock the door behind me."

Her throat tightened a little. They both were acutely aware of the danger she faced 24/7. After Harlan left, she returned her attention to the security screen. Two more cars with news logos on the side pulled into the lot. She watched the screen, hoping, praying, that it would be Jackson and Smokey standing by the podium with her.

A dog and his handler came on-screen— Vivienne Armstrong and her border collie, Hank. Then a second K-9 pair, Detective Bradley McGregor and his Malinois, King, came into view. They were followed by Belle Montera and her German shepherd, Justice. Finally, Jackson and Smokey appeared on-screen, as well. Darcy thought she might cry. They really did have her back.

She watched as the two female officers stopped the first reporters before they could enter the building. Vivienne, Hank heeled at her side, checked their credentials and did a pat-down for weapons before the reporters were allowed to enter. Belle and Justice stood by. Darcy knew from having interacted with the K-9 Unit that Justice was trained for protection.

A few minutes later, there were five knocks on the lab door, three fast and two slow. Jackson's code. She pressed the security code to unlock the door.

Jackson, dressed in full uniform, stood there with Smokey. "I'm here to escort you to the conference room," he said, adding, "One officer and his K-9 are in place in the room already. King, Detective McGregor's Malinois, is trained in protection, so you are in good hands. Officer Vivienne Armstrong and Hank, along with Belle Montera and Justice, will guard the outside door, controlling who gets in."

Her heart swelled with gratitude. "I saw how many officers showed up to help. Thanks, Jackson."

She stepped out, making sure the lab was locked behind her. Jackson had thought of everything to keep her safe.

She smoothed over the front of her tan blazer

and then glanced down at her polka-dotted pumps. The shoes made her smile.

They walked together down the hall. All eyes were on her as she entered the room and took her place behind the podium. Jackson and Smokey stood to one side, while Bradley and King were positioned by the door.

Darcy laced her hands together and rested them on the podium. She looked out at the eager faces waiting for her to speak and took in a breath that she hoped would quiet her turbulent stomach.

"As you know, the killer of Griffin Martel is still at large. We had a breakthrough in the case today. On the night the body was located, Officer Davison of the Brooklyn K-9 Unit found a gun in a nearby trash can, after chasing an unknown person who'd been hiding in the foliage near the victim. We don't know if that person was involved in the homicide of Mr. Martel or who the gun belonged to, but we do know it was the murder weapon." She turned her head slightly toward Jackson and Smokey.

Ever the professionals, they both stood at attention, focusing on the crowd of gathered reporters.

She looked out at the journalists while cameras flashed. "The bullet that killed Griffin

Martel is a match for the gun we found. The gun was not registered, which means it was probably obtained illegally." She stared down at the podium for a moment before taking a breath and looking up. "There was a set of prints found on the gun. Those prints belong to Reuben Bray."

She braced for the barrage of questions and accusations.

"Aren't you set to testify in his trial this week?"

"Yes," she said. Her heart raced and her stomach felt like it had rock in it.

"How can a man sitting in a prison cell commit a murder?"

"He can't." Darcy knew she wasn't allowed to offer her theory that she was being set up to look like she couldn't do her job. She had to deal in the facts. She reiterated the evidence that had initially led to Reuben's indictment for murder.

"Do you think you might have made in a mistake analyzing the evidence that sent Reuben Bray to jail for murder in the first place?"

"No, I do not."

A female reporter, who Darcy recognized from a regional television station, took two steps toward her. "Miss Fields, since the Brooklyn K-9 Unit was involved in Reuben

Bray's initial capture, maybe you were feeling some pressure from them to bring forth some evidence to put him away."

"That is not the case." Her voice rose half an octave. She swallowed and gripped the sides of the podium to try to regain control of her emotions. Out of the corner of her eye, she saw Jackson twitch. The accusation bothered him, too. "I assure you that Forensics works with all of the units in the NYPD with the utmost integrity."

A male reporter interjected, "So the trial of Reuben Bray will go forward?"

Motion at the back of the room by the door caught Darcy's attention. A blonde stepped out from behind a camera being operated by a man. She looked right at Darcy and then stepped through the door. A chill ran down Darcy's spine.

"Miss Fields? Are you going to answer the question?" another reporter called out.

The blond woman had been dressed in a suit and had a press pass around her neck. The look she had given Darcy had been filled with malice. Darcy's heart raged in her chest.

Jackson must have picked up on her alarm. He and Smokey moved toward her and, wrapping his arm across her back, Jackson led her away from the podium. "I think Miss Fields has answered enough questions today."

"You're from the Brooklyn K-9 Unit, aren't you? You and Miss Fields seem very cozy," a female reporter, who Darcy knew to be from a local newspaper, quipped.

Jackson's jaw turned to granite. "Miss Fields has had threats against her life. She requires protection."

One of the reporters spoke under his breath. "This whole thing stinks of collusion."

More than anything, Darcy wanted to respond to the accusation, but she knew silence was the more professional choice.

Jackson led her through the crowded room toward the conference room door as the peppering of questions continued. Smokey remained close. Once they were in the hallway, the reporters followed them to the lab.

Harlan was waiting for them, holding the lab door open. They slipped inside while the lab tech stood in the hallway to answer the reporters' questions.

Darcy turned to face him. "Jackson, I saw her. She was at the news conference at the back of the room. I know it was her." It had been at least five minutes since the woman had left the room. There had been no opportunity to tell him earlier with the reporters crowding them.

Jackson's eyes grew wide. He pressed the call button on his radio. "Suspect on the run just outside the forensics lab." He clicked off the radio. "What did she look like?"

"Blond, dressed in a navy suit. Press pass."

Jackson relayed the information.

She could still hear the commotion of the reporters on the other side of the door though it sounded like it was dying down a little.

Darcy glanced at the surveillance screen. Some of the news vans were pulling out of the parking lot. She watched as Vivienne ran across the lot with Hank and disappeared.

A moment later, her voice came across Jackson's radio. "I found a blond wig and a press pass in the garbage."

"She's probably long gone." Darcy sighed, trying not to give in to despair. She had a feeling the woman had also been wearing a wig when she'd thrown off the baseball cap after fleeing the museum. The Manhattan forensics lab was testing it for DNA, but Darcy didn't hold out too much hope that the perp would be ID'd that way.

"We're not giving up that easily," Jackson said. "At least we can use the wig to put the tracking dog onto her. If she's close by and hasn't gotten into a car, we might still have a chance at catching her. She might be hid-

"Darcy, how good to see you. And I see you brought a friend." Reuben offered her a hundred-watt smile.

The press might be taken in by his good looks and charm, but Jackson could barely contain his irritation. The guy was a slimy manipulator.

Darcy's stern expression suggested she wasn't fooled by his act, either.

"I'm sure you heard—or maybe you already knew—that we found your prints on the gun that killed Griffin Martel."

Again, Rueben grinned. "Wow, that's interesting." He sat back in his chair, crossed his arms over his chest and leered at her. "How could that happen? I've been in this jail cell the whole time." His tone became sarcastic. "Are you sure you did the fingerprint test right, Darcy?"

Jackson leaned forward, his hand balled into fist. "Her name is Miss Fields."

"Look, Rueben," Darcy said, "the judge ade the decision to move forward with your al."

curtain seemed to drop over Rueben's res and he pressed his lips together. The ge was subtle, but Jackson was good at ng body language. Darcy's news about al going forward had upset him.

ing somewhere close waiting for her chance to get at you."

Darcy allowed a realization to sink in. "I think all of this is connected to Reuben Bray and his trial. The gun was planted to make me look incompetent. And that woman…" She shook her head. "I think she's trying to stop the trial either by getting it thrown out or by killing me."

"You might be right," Jackson conceded. "One thing is for sure. We have to get out to Rikers and talk to Reuben Bray. We need to find out who she is and if she has a connection to Reuben."

"Let's go," Darcy said.

They passed through the door as Harlan entered the lab. A trickle of reporters remained in the hallway and in the parking lot. As they hurried to Jackson's SUV, some continued to snap pictures of Jackson and Darcy together. Darcy knew she couldn't control the press's fixated narrative, though it bothered her that a cloud had shadowed her work and that of the Brooklyn K-9 Unit for unfair reasons.

TWELVE

After informing Dispatch where he was going and why, Jackson focused on driving to the prison. The report came across his radio that the search for the woman Darcy had seen at the press conference had yielded nothing.

That meant she was still at large. The tracking dogs would have located her if she had remained anywhere close. As long as she was out there, he had to assume that they both were still under threat.

Darcy's phone rang. She clicked it on and gave short one-word answers to whomever she was talking to on the other end of the line. "Thanks, Harlan." She ended the call and told Jackson, "So the judge was informed about the fingerprints on the gun before I held the press conference. He just sent us a response. He wants to go forward with Reuben's trial. He regards the Griffin Martel murder as a separate case." He picked up on the distress in

Darcy's voice. She turned and stared out the window.

"Legally, that's true, but the press won't treat it that way."

Once they arrived at Rikers, they left Smokey in the SUV with the air-conditioning on and the doors locked, a feature he appreciated, and walked across the parking lot to the entrance of the prison.

Jackson explained to the desk clerk that they needed to speak to Rueben Bray. They were searched and led through a series of security gates into a room where they were instructed to sit at a desk separated by a wall of glass with another desk on the other side. Rueben was only allowed non-contact visits. Less violent prisoners could sit at a table with their loved ones and lawyers. There were at least te visitor stations in this room. Only one stati on the far side was occupied by a gray-ha woman who clutched her purse and spo a twentysomething man on the other the glass.

Jackson retrieved a second chair. Darcy's hand where it rested on the glanced at him, smiling. A door a the room opened and Rueben corted by a guard. He took his s opposite them. The guard stoo

"Whatever you and your female accomplice were hoping to sabotage by planting that gun didn't work," Jackson said.

Rueben's brows knit together. "I don't know what you're talking about." He burst to his feet. "I'm done here. I want to go back to my cell."

They waited until Rueben and the guard disappeared behind the door.

"He tried to hide it, but I think we're onto something," Jackson said. "Let's go check the visitor logs to find out who's been to see him."

They left the visitation room and returned to the front desk where they had signed in before seeing Rueben. "We need to know who has been coming to see Rueben Bray," Jackson told the clerk.

The clerk pulled out a computer notebook and typed something before sliding the notebook across the counter.

Jackson looked at the names and dates.

Darcy stared over his shoulder.

Several of the names also had the last name "Bray."

"Maybe it's not a girlfriend. Maybe it's a sister who's been doing his dirty work or some other relative," Darcy suggested.

"Could be," Jackson said.

Darcy pointed to some of the names on the list. "That one is a reporter and so is that one."

Both the names were female.

"You said the perp wore a press pass at the lab—it could have been a fake or maybe she's one of these reporters. Do you think she might be involved with him?"

"Maybe." Darcy pointed to one of the names and shook her head. "This woman is like fifty and she's a really good journalist. The other one is Rueben's age." Darcy flipped the page and scanned it. "Looks like she's been here only three times in the last month, though. But she is a possibility. The press pass was probably a fake."

Darcy pulled out her phone and recorded the name on her virtual notebook.

Jackson continued to look for any repeat names. "What about this one? Chloe Cleaves?"

"It's not a name I recognize. Looks like she visits at least once a week."

"Let's start with her," Jackson said. "I'll phone into headquarters. Eden Chang, our tech expert, can input her name to see if she has a record."

"We can find out if the guard who usually is on duty during visiting hours is here. They watch the interaction between prisoners and visitors. He might have some insight into the nature of their relationship and could tell us what she looks like."

Jackson shook his head. "Your mind really does work like a detective's."

Darcy's face brightened at the compliment. "I'll stick to the lab."

It took them only a few minutes to track down a guard who had watched most of Rueben's interactions with his visitors. He met them at the entrance to the prison. They asked about family members and then the reporters.

The guard rubbed his bald spot. "He has had his share of reporters show up, but I wouldn't say they were here for anything but a story or a statement from him."

"And what about Chloe Cleaves?" Darcy asked.

The guard let out a heavy breath and nodded. "She's here a lot. Even though the visits are 'no contact,' everything about her body language says they're involved."

Jackson leaned a little closer to the prison guard. He felt a sense of excitement. They were on the right track. "What does she look like?"

"Dark brown hair. Slender. Not a lot of makeup. Usually has her hair braided. You know, that fancy way," said the guard.

"You mean a French braid," Darcy said.

The guard nodded. "I guess."

They thanked the man and returned to the K-9 vehicle. Jackson opened the back door. "I need to take Smokey for a quick walk. Why don't you get in and lock the doors? I won't go far."

He walked Smokey to the edge of the parking lot. When he looked over his shoulder, Darcy was sitting in the passenger seat staring in his direction.

There was something in her expression that suggested a deep level of trust. These small moments—a look on her face or her hand brushing over his—brought light into his day. Somehow she'd managed to chip away at the stone around his heart. Not what he had counted on at all.

After a few minutes, Jackson returned to the SUV and loaded his partner in the back. Before he got in himself, he had a look around. After seeing Rueben, they had spent at least another half hour in the prison getting information. He didn't know what kind of communication privileges Rueben had, but a half hour would have been plenty of time for him to alert whoever was doing his bidding on the outside that they were at Rikers.

Jackson got into his vehicle and pulled out of the lot just as Eden Chang's voice came on the radio.

"Hey, Jackson. I pulled up the sheet on Chloe Cleaves."

"So, she has a record?"

"A recent arrest for prescription drug abuse. But wait, there's more!" Eden's bright voice came across the line.

"What else did you find out?"

"I did a quick search of her name. It's unusual enough, I thought something might come up."

"And you found something interesting, right?" Jackson prompted. "We wouldn't be talking if you hadn't."

"She hasn't posted on her Facebook for well over a year, but Chloe used to be in training for the biathlon."

"Really, a biathlon?"

Darcy sat up in her seat and looked at Jackson.

Eden continued. "And guess who one of her assistant coaches used to be?"

"Not Rueben Bray?" Jackson couldn't picture Rueben as the athletic type. He was mostly an unemployed hustler and purse snatcher.

"No, but one of her coaches was Griffin Martel. He looked familiar in the group photo she posted, so I ran it through some facial recognition software. He lost his job as a coach when he was arrested for selling prescription drugs to the athletes."

"You have no idea how much that helps us."

"I don't know why she would have killed Martel. Surely not just to plant a gun with Reuben's prints on it to discredit Darcy," the tech guru said. "And I can't find how she knows Reuben. He's not anywhere on her Facebook page."

"Reuben was in constant trouble with the law. If she was in trouble, too, they might have crossed paths in a courthouse or some other place connected with being arrested," Jackson said.

"That would be my theory, too."

"Good work. Thanks, Eden. I'm assuming it was easy to pull a current address on her?"

"Yes. I had Dispatch send a patrol car over there to bring her in for questioning."

He doubted that Chloe would be home, but it was a place to start. Because of her connection to Rueben, she was a person of interest. At the very least they needed to talk to her.

He clicked off his radio. He relayed the information Eden had given him to Darcy.

"I finally feel like we're getting somewhere," said Darcy. "A biathlete shoots a rifle and then skis. That could explain our shooter's marksmanship skills and why she's so athletic."

"Chloe's looking pretty good for our suspect."

He turned up the street that led to the long

bridge connecting Rikers Island to Queens. Only buses and authorized vehicles could travel on the girded structure. He could see LaGuardia Airport through his side window.

Dispatch came over the radio. "Chloe Cleaves is not at her apartment, but we have a patrol officer parked outside in case she does show."

"Not surprised," Jackson said to Darcy.

They were almost to the end of the bridge when the windshield of the SUV turned into a thousand tiny pieces. On reflex, he lifted his hand to protect his eyes from possible flying shards.

They'd been shot at.

"Get down!" he shouted at Darcy.

A horn honked as Jackson inadvertently swerved into oncoming traffic. He overcorrected. The SUV hit the guardrail, slid for several feet, then broke through and fell into the East River.

Darcy's vision blurred. The impact of hitting the water had left her disoriented. Her whole body seemed to be shaking. Jackson's voice brought her back to reality. The SUV was sinking.

"Get out," Jackson said.

The passenger's-side window was nearly

submerged. It was too late to try to get out that way. She unfastened her seat belt, knowing not to try to escape through the door until the car was covered in water so there would be equal pressure inside and out.

Jackson had already released of his seat belt and had turned to reach for the latch on Smokey's crate to free him.

Heart racing, blood pumping, she fumbled for her door handle. Once the latch released, Darcy turned and pushed with her feet, knowing it would take effort to open the door. She squeezed through and swam upward. The cold water of the East River presented a challenge as she stroked her arms and kicked her legs. She bobbed to the surface, gasping for air, and turning her head one way and then the other. She didn't see Jackson or Smokey.

People had begun to gather on shore. She heard sirens in the distance.

The waters were turbulent and she had to work hard to keep her head above the waves. She could feel the cold seeping in. A boat with the Coast Guard insignia was moving at a steady pace toward her.

She turned her head, searching for Jackson and Smokey, and feeling a rising panic.

Dear God, please say they made it.

Suddenly she caught sight of an object so

dark, it was almost the same color as the water. Smokey swam toward her.

Fear gripped her heart.

What if Jackson had drowned?

All she could see was the black churning water all around. Then some distance away from where she and Smokey had come up, she saw Jackson's head.

She breathed a sigh of relief as he swam toward her. His muscular arms cut through the roiling water as if it were nothing.

"We made it," he said as he reached her and Smokey. "All three of us."

As the Coast Guard boat drew near, Darcy swam the short distance to it and waited to be towed in while she clutched the life preserver. Once on board, a blanket was thrown over her and a Coast Guard ensign tossed the life ring out again. Jackson wrapped an arm around Smokey so they could be towed in together.

Jackson climbed on board. He addressed one of the Coast Guard members who threw a blanket over Smokey and offered him one. "I need to use your radio. We were shot at. Mostly likely from those trees that surround the Little League park. We need to do a search and get a lockdown in the area as quickly as possible before the shooter disappears into the city."

Still clutching her own blanket, Darcy

rubbed Smokey with his to dry him off. The dog turned and licked her face. She was shivering and so was Smokey. Jackson seemed unfazed by the accident and submersion into cold water.

"We can do that," said the young Coast Guard ensign. He touched Jackson's arm. "Sir, you may have suffered a degree of hypothermia. You need to focus on warming your core temperature. There are places belowdecks for the two of you to change into dry clothes."

Jackson paced as water dripped off his uniform and hair. His radio was most likely too waterlogged to work. "We need a thorough search of the entire area. We have wasted precious minutes."

"Yes, sir," said the ensign. "We'll radio that message to the shore right away if you will focus on getting warm and dry."

Jackson seemed to be still running on adrenaline. Darcy shivered as she stepped up to him and took his hand. "He's right, Jackson. We need to take care of ourselves. Our bodies have had a terrible shock."

Jackson turned and looked at her.

"They'll take care of the search. You're not good to anyone like this."

He shook his head. "You're right. I just don't want her to get away."

They were escorted belowdecks by a female member of the Coast Guard who showed them where to change. Before she headed back toward the ladder that led topside, she pointed to a narrow counter space that held a coffeemaker and microwave. "You can make yourself a cup of tea or coffee once you get out of those wet clothes."

Darcy changed into the sweats the Coast Guard provided. Once she stepped out, Smokey was waiting for her. "Jackson?" He must have gone above deck. His focus was on catching the woman who had almost killed all three of them.

"Come here, Smokey." The K-9 wagged his tail and stepped over to her. She wrapped her arms around the chocolate Lab, glad his shivering had stopped. "I'm so glad we all made it." She held the dog close.

Chloe Cleaves had to be the one behind the attacks. She had a motive for wanting Darcy dead. She didn't want her to testify at Reuben's trial. Who else would have known they would be on that bridge at that time? Rueben must have contacted her so she could get into place and wait. Every call from jail would be traced. Maybe Rueben had phoned someone who'd then contacted Chloe. She could only guess at how the message had been transmitted.

Unless the police caught Chloe today, it was just a matter of time before she came after Darcy again.

Darcy held Smokey close, fighting off the fear that threatened to overwhelm her.

THIRTEEN

Jackson paced the deck of the Coast Guard boat as they drew near to shore. He saw at least five police cars, thinking they must be from the Queens precinct to have gotten there so quickly. Unless Chloe'd had a car waiting for her, she was probably still close by. Darcy had only seen her a few hours ago at the press conference. She probably hadn't had time to make arrangements for a getaway car and driver. The boat drew close to the dock.

Darcy and Smokey came up on deck. Her hair was still wet, but the color had come back into her cheeks. Smokey had mostly dried off.

Jackson stepped toward her. "When we get to shore, I need you to stay in one of the police cars until Smokey and I come for you. Chloe is probably still around here. She might decide to take another shot at you. I'll make sure there is an officer close by to watch over you. Do you understand?"

She nodded and looked up at him. The affection that radiated from her expression moved him deeply.

"Smokey and I are going to find her." He rested his hand on her cheek. "I want this to be over for you."

"And for you, too," she said.

The boat jerked slightly as it slipped into the dock. He fell toward her, catching himself in her arms. His lips found hers and he kissed her. As she wrapped her arms around his neck, he deepened the kiss. All the uncertainty seemed to fall away when he held her. She remained close and he kissed her head.

"It's going to be okay," he said. "I promise."

She rested her forehead against his and gripped is collar. "I know it will be, Jackson."

With the electric energy of the kiss still making his head buzz, they disembarked and Jackson escorted her to a police car in the parking lot by the dock.

Jackson opened the back door of the patrol car for Darcy. She got in and gazed up at him.

Resting his arm on the door, he leaned in a little closer to her. "This is the safest place for you." He reached over and brushed her chin with his knuckles.

She smiled up at him before closing the door. With Smokey heeled beside him—Smokey's leash had been lost in the sunken police vehicle—Jackson made his way over to a patrol officer. "I'm here to help with the search," he told him, taking his badge out of the pocket of his sweats to show it to the officer. Though his radio was no good, he had put his utility belt with his firearm back on.

"We need all the help we can get," said the officer.

Jackson pointed to the police car where Darcy waited. "Can you keep an eye on her?"

"Sure, no problem," said the officer. "I'm watching the parking lot and the area around it in case the shooter comes this way. Two of our guys went through the trees toward the Little League field, one went up toward 19th Avenue, and the other is searching the parking lot through the trees on the other side of the street."

Because Jackson was without a radio, he wouldn't be able to communicate with the other officers, which would hinder him. "If the shooter makes it to 19th Avenue, we have a strong indication the shooter is female with an athletic build. If we don't catch her, she could disappear into the crowded neighborhood of Astoria even if she was still on foot. Are K-9 officers on the way so we can search the city streets, as well?"

"Officers are getting here as fast as they can. Some are even heading over from the Brooklyn unit. Right now, we have patrol officers on the ground."

It made sense to search the immediate area first. "Thanks. Can you please radio the patrol officers headed toward the baseball field that I'm joining the search with my dog, so they don't hear me coming and think I'm the fugitive?"

The other officer nodded.

Jackson took off at a dead run toward where he thought the shots had come from.

He sprinted through the band of trees that bordered the baseball fields. Smokey ran close to him.

Noises to the side caused him to stop. Another officer emerged through the trees.

Jackson held up his badge. "I'm Officer Davison."

The officer, a forty-something man built like a football player, nodded. "I heard over the radio you were helping out. We need all the manpower we can get. Some other officers are working 80th Street by the water. A few of us have the trees on this side covered. If you want to head through the Little League field toward Bowery Bay, we will have this area covered. If we don't locate the shooter, we'll push the search into Manhattan. Patrol cars are on their way to help with that."

Jackson nodded. "Once I get to the edge of the field, I'm going to cut toward 19th. My guess is she's going to try to get to where people are as fast as she can."

"Or she'll find a hiding place close to the water. She'd have to be running pretty fast to get to 19th Avenue."

"Don't underestimate her. She's very athletic," Jackson said.

The Queens' officer disappeared into the trees while Jackson ran the other way. Within minutes, the K-9 team was clear of the trees. Jackson's feet pounded across the baseball diamonds as he looked side to side. Up ahead was another cluster of trees where 80th Street and 19th Avenue intersected.

Sirens wailed in the distance. More help was on the way. Smokey picked up the pace as they got closer to the trees. He must have detected something.

They entered the treed area. Jackson could hear the hum of traffic on 19th Avenue not far away. A closer noise drew his attention back to the trees. He and Smokey headed in that direction.

He stopped when something shiny on the ground caught his attention. The rifle. Chloe must have ditched it because she'd be too easy to spot hauling it on the street. That meant she was panicked and close by.

With Smokey's help, he did a quick search for her in the area where the rifle had been dropped then raced toward the street. Once clear of the trees, his view was of cars, streets, people and buildings. He scanned everywhere, locking on to the face of every pedestrian. All she had to do was blend in and not call attention to herself. He tried to get a look at the people in the cars, as well.

Not wanting to be slowed down by carrying the rifle, Jackson continued his search, running for several blocks before giving up. The smart thing to do would be to get the rifle before someone snatched it, so it could be taken into evidence. He also needed to find a cop with a radio so the other officers could shift their search parameters, though now that Chloe was in the city, the chances of catching her were substantially reduced.

He went back to where the rifle was, conducting an even deeper search of the area on the outside chance Chloe had returned. He found nothing.

As he carried the rifle, Jackson gritted his teeth. A sense of frustration overtook him. At least Chloe couldn't shoot from a distance anymore. That just meant she would find some other way to get to Darcy.

Darcy sat in the back of the patrol car wishing she could be helping in some way. Several calls came over the radio, indicating that the police had completed searches of different areas without finding Chloe and that more officers were arriving.

The patrol officer paced through the parking lot and searched the edges of it. He looked in Darcy's direction every five minutes. She waited, staring at the ceiling.

Another call came over the police radio. A rifle had been found, but still no shooter.

Darcy tapped her fingers on the seat.

Her phone rang. Good, it still worked. She was glad she'd sprung for the waterproof model. The number was Harlan's, not Jackson's. She quelled her disappointment.

"Hey, Harlan. What's up?"

"Darcy, have you been watching the news?"

"No, I've been a bit preoccupied."

"Maybe it's better that way." Harlan sounded distressed.

"What's going on?"

"Look, this was not my decision. But I asked to be the one to break the news to you even though I'm not your boss."

Darcy felt that familiar twisting knot in her stomach. "Don't drag it out. Just tell me."

"This whole thing with Reuben and the gun found at the Martel crime scene... The press won't let go of the idea that the K-9 Unit put pressure on Forensics to come up with evidence that linked the first murder to Reuben Bray."

This was not news to her. "Harlan, tell me something I don't already know." She knew Harlan was probably taking a long time to get to the point because he cared about her feelings.

"The higher-ups think it would be good if you went on paid leave until the air clears over this. They will make a statement and there will be an investigation into the allegations. I know that you are good at your job. They think once Reuben's trial takes place, and the details get out to the press, this will blow over. You're always amazing on the stand, Darcy," he said. "The trial will be televised. People will know you would never be sloppy in your work or cave to pressure from anyone."

Her throat went tight. "Okay, I guess if that's how it has to be."

"Darcy, I'm really sorry about this."

"It's not your fault. The trial will go forward, and people will see the truth." She ended the call, determined not to give in to negative thoughts. The thing that bothered her the most was that her work on the Emery case would be put on the back burner again.

Someone tapped on her window.

She started, not realizing how deep in thought she'd been. It was Jackson, Smokey heeled at his side.

She rolled down the window, noting Jackson's grim expression. "I heard on the radio what happened. At least she doesn't have a rifle anymore."

He nodded. "Since it is only a strong theory that Chloe is behind all this... If the rifle can be linked to her, it won't be just a theory anymore."

"That's how cases get solved. One piece of evidence at a time." She tried to sound hopeful.

Jackson shook his head. "Look, I'm going to see if I can get a patrol car to take us back to your apartment. I'll clear the place and stay with you until an officer is parked outside. I'm kind of useless without a radio anyway. I do need to swing by somewhere and get a temp phone. Too dangerous to be without one."

She heard the despair in his voice. She felt it, too.

When would this be over?

FOURTEEN

Jackson awoke in Darcy's dark living room to Smokey's low-level growl.

He'd fallen asleep on her couch. When it looked like the department couldn't spare a patrol car to sit outside for several hours, he'd opted to stay with her, especially because her sister was away on another school trip and Darcy would be alone. The plunge into the river had caught up with both of them. Darcy had gone to sleep in her room, and he had conked out, as well, falling into a deep sleep.

Jackson reached out to touch Smokey where he lay on the floor by the couch. "What is it, boy?" It could just be a loud noise on the street that had alarmed Smokey.

All the same, Jackson needed to check it out. Except for a light from the kitchen, which was bright enough to see by, the room was dark.

He sat up. The shades on Darcy's repaired window had been drawn. Feeling rested, he rose and walked across the room, pulling the curtain back so he had a view of the street. Though it was past ten, the neighborhood was still very much alive at this time of night. Traffic, though sparse, clipped by on the street. Behind him, Smokey was still agitated.

Jackson moved down the hallway, padding softly. He eased Darcy's door open just a crack to make sure she was okay. The night-light illuminated her sleeping form, Mr. Tubbs next to her.

It was still at least an hour before the patrol division would have an officer available to protect Darcy. He stepped back down the hall and returned to the living room/kitchen area. He stopped by the couch. Though he could not say why, something had shifted since he'd left the room. The hairs on the back of his neck stood at attention. His heartbeat thrummed in his ears. He couldn't see or hear Smokey.

He stepped closer to the kitchen. His dog lay on his side, motionless.

He barely had time to register the blow to the back of his head before he crumpled to the ground unconscious.

Darcy awoke with as start in total darkness. Her night-light had stopped working. Mr.

Tubbs leaped off the bed, making a yowling noise that indicated distress.

Darcy sat up, waiting for her eyes to adjust to the darkness and for the fog of sleep to lift. As she rose from the bed, her heart beat a little faster. Maybe it was just the darkness that was making her so afraid.

Now that she was more awake, she could find her way to the light switch in the dark. She took several steps on the carpet, holding her hand out in front of her. She stepped carefully over the objects on the floor. Her hand found the wall and then the light switch.

Just as the room lit up, she saw that her night-light had been pulled out of the outlet. Before what that meant could even register in her brain, a hand went over her mouth.

The person who had grabbed her was a woman. A very strong woman. Darcy felt herself being dragged backward. She twisted to try to free herself. She struggled with such force that she got away but fell on the floor on her stomach.

She crawled on all fours to escape. Then flipped over. The woman stepped toward Darcy, her face red, teeth showing. Chloe.

Chloe pulled a Taser out of her pocket.

Darcy yelled out Jackson's name twice. Chloe stalked toward her, weapon in hand.

Darcy reached for the first object her hand could find—a boot, which she threw at the other woman. She hit her mark, smacking Chloe in the head, causing her to drop the Taser.

Frantic, Darcy glanced around for another object to throw. She turned over and crawled toward the other boot, which she threw, hitting Chloe in the stomach. The distraction gave Darcy time to stand. She grabbed everything she could, hurling it all at her attacker: a curling iron, a hairbrush, makeup. Chloe held her hands up in a defensive posture. Darcy's caught sight of the Taser on the floor, but there was no way she could get to it in time.

Chloe's eyes were filled with murderous rage as she lunged toward Darcy.

Darcy jumped on the bed, thinking something must have happened to Jackson or he would have come by now. There was now only one way out of the bedroom. Chloe was closer to the door than Darcy was. She couldn't get out that way without being caught. Maybe she could fling the window open and yell for help at least. She wouldn't be able to get out because of the bars. She slid off the bed and reached for the latch.

Chloe grabbed her from behind, yanking her pajama shirt back so hard that the collar dug into her neck. Darcy twisted, trying to break free. She kicked wildly, not making impact with anything.

Chloe spun her around and grabbed her neck under the chin with one hand.

Darcy choked and gasped for air as Chloe pressed on her windpipe. Black dots filled Darcy's field of vision. Chloe used her free hand to pull a sheathed knife from her back pocket.

Air. Darcy needed air. It would be easier for Chloe to kill her with the knife if she was unconscious and couldn't fight back. Chloe's original intent must have been to disable her with the Taser and then stab her.

Chloe let go of Darcy to pull the sheath off the knife. Darcy gasped and sputtered. She bent over, wheezing in air. When she looked up, the knife blade caught the light.

Fear enveloped her at the same time an instinct to survive kicked into high gear. She had to get away.

Darcy took a step toward Chloe, intending to push her out of the way so she could get to the bedroom door. Chloe pointed the knife at her, causing her to freeze. Darcy reached for the hand that held the knife, but Chloe was faster and stronger.

She knocked Darcy's hand away and grabbed her throat again, squeezing as she backed her up to a wall. Though she could get some breath, Darcy was growing light-headed.

Chloe raised the knife.

Darcy clawed at the hand that held her neck at the same time that she angled her body with all the force she could muster.

She felt a slice of pain on her upper arm and then the warm ooze of blood. She reached a hand out to push Chloe out of the way. The blade went into her stomach.

This is not happening.

The sound of Smokey's barking seemed to come from very far away.

A look of shock clouded Chloe's expression. She turned and ran out of the room.

Darcy looked down at the red drops of blood on her floor. She turned away, seeking to protect herself, pressing her hand against the expanding red circle on her stomach as she doubled over.

Her vision narrowed to a pinpoint. She was losing consciousness.

She was going down.

Her head hit the corner of the dresser.

As her world went black, a thought cascaded through her mind.

I'm going to die here.

FIFTEEN

As Jackson regained consciousness, the first thing to register was that Smokey was barking and pacing around him, clearly upset that Jackson was lying on the floor, not moving. Fear seized his heart. Chloe must have knocked him unconscious to get to Darcy. He could only guess at what she had used to disable Smokey. He pushed himself to his feet, swaying as his head throbbed with pain. He hurried through the living room. He heard banging noises. And then silence. He pulled his weapon and stepped down the hallway seeing a very scared cat seek refuge in the other bedroom.

A breeze from the open bathroom door caused him to peer inside. A window had been left open. The only window that didn't have bars across it. That must have been how Chloe had gotten in, despite the lock.

His primary concern was for Darcy. He ran to her bedroom, pulling his phone out.

He dialed headquarters and advised Gavin of Chloe's possible location.

He pushed the door open. Darcy lay face-down on the floor, not moving. His breathing became shallow as he ran over to her. Kneeling, he turned her over. She was unresponsive. She had a bleeding gash on her forehead and her upper arm had been cut, but it was the stain of blood on her pajama shirt that made him gasp. The side of her neck pulsed. She was alive but unconscious and losing a lot of blood. He still had Gavin on the line. "Get an ambulance to Darcy's address."

Smokey's barking must have caused Chloe to flee before she'd had a chance to stab Darcy with the fatal blow. She must have been concerned about getting in and out quickly or she would have taken the time to kill him and Smokey, too. He saw the Taser on the floor—no doubt that had disabled Smokey long enough for Chloe to have hit Jackson on the back of the head.

There were bruises on Darcy's neck, consistent with someone trying to strangle her. The gash on her forehead suggested she had been hit by an object. The blow was probably what had knocked her out.

"Come on, Darcy," he said. He drew her

closer to his chest and whispered in her ear. "Come back to me. I don't want to lose you."

He heard the paramedics knocking on the locked front door. He ran to let them in.

Within minutes, they had taken Darcy's vitals and loaded her on a stretcher. She had not regained consciousness. Jackson stood back, feeling helpless as they wheeled her outside. He didn't want to leave Smokey behind and the K-9 couldn't ride in the ambulance. "I'll catch a ride and follow you guys."

Several police units were now in the area searching for Chloe. Jackson chased down one of the officers and asked to use the patrol car. He secured Smokey in the passenger seat. Smokey whined and licked Jackson's cheeks.

"She's in a real tough spot, Smokey."

Jackson pulled out onto the street. Focusing in on the flashing lights of the ambulance, he sped up. The ambulance remained several blocks ahead of him all the way to the emergency room. By the time he found a parking space, Darcy had been unloaded and was being transported into the ER. He got behind the stretcher and followed it into the exam area.

A curtain was pulled around her. He watched as doctors and other medical staff entered her cubicle. He could hear their chatter and medical jargon.

His heart squeezed tight. He stepped toward where the curtain was open a sliver.

A nurse stepped up to him from inside the cubicle. "Sir, are you family?"

"No, I'm a friend. A good friend."

"Why don't you take a chair and we'll let you know as soon as we can what the prognosis is for her. We need to stabilize her and get that cut in abdomen stitched up."

"I can't sit still. I'll check back in a few minutes." He stepped outside into the chill September night. Jackson walked over to his loaner patrol car, opened the door and commanded Smokey to jump down.

He couldn't shake off his nerves and worry over what was going to happen with Darcy. Seeing her so lifeless in that unconscious state had really shaken him. With Smokey next to him, he did a brisk walk that turned into a run. As his steps ate up distance over both sidewalk and grass, he prayed for Darcy's recovery.

She was part of his life now. A big part.

In addition to how fun she was, the nice thing about Darcy was that she understood what it meant to be a police officer. The kiss they'd shared had been a little impulsive, but that didn't mean he hadn't liked kissing her. His feelings for her were such a tangled mess. In his heart, he knew that friendship was the kindest thing he could offer Darcy. If he was still on guard from the wounds of his last relationship, he wouldn't be any good to her as a boyfriend. If there was to be anything between them, he had to know that he could give 100 percent. What did it matter anyway? She didn't date cops.

His run slowed to a walk. He'd gone completely around the hospital and his car was now in sight. He loaded Smokey back into the vehicle, put the air-conditioning on low and locked the car, again grateful for that feature because he didn't know how long he'd be inside. He was just turning back toward the ER entrance when he noticed a hunched-over figure in baggy clothes disappear inside.

Would Chloe be so bold as to show up here? It would be easy enough to conclude that Darcy had ended up in the hospital even if Chloe hadn't hidden somewhere to watch what had happened.

His heart beat a little faster and he sprinted across the parking lot to the ER entrance. When he stepped inside the brightly lit room, he saw no one in the waiting area who resembled the hooded figure.

Jackson walked the aisles of the ER, past pulled curtains, a closed door where a man groaned in agony, and past another partially open door where he heard a child crying. He widened his search, stepping toward the elevators. He had nothing to go on but his gut instinct. The hooded figure reminded him of the watcher in the woods when he and Smokey had found Griffin Martel's body.

She's here.

Jackson headed for the ER as he pulled his phone out and pressed Gavin's number which he had memorized.

Gavin picked up right away. "Jackson. How is she?"

"I don't know. The doctors haven't said anything. The cut in her stomach looked pretty bad and she suffered a blow to the head. I'm sure she'll be admitted. We need to get her some protection. I'll stay with her until an officer can be put outside her hospital door."

"Give me a couple of hours. I'm pretty sure we can put something like that in place given the level of threat against her," Gavin said.

"It wouldn't hurt to do a search of the hospital," Jackson suggested.

"You have some evidence that Chloe may be hiding in the hospital?"

"Just a hunch based on her past behavior."

"Jackson, I understand your concern, but I can't send officers over on a hunch. We're stretched thin as it is combing the city for her.

Because of the past attacks and Chloe being at large again, I acknowledge that Darcy is in significant danger. It makes sense to have some protection for her. That is the best that I can do right now."

"I understand," Jackson said.

"We're looking into all her known associates besides Reuben Bray," Gavin told him. "She may be staying with one of them. She's from upstate and has no relatives in the area. We believe that as long as Darcy is alive and Reuben Bray's trial goes forward, she will stay in the city. I'll let you know if we get any leads. Also, we got a warrant to search her place. We recovered a handgun."

No wonder Chloe had used a knife and Taser. "What else can we do, right? Thanks, Sarge." Jackson shut off his phone and wandered back to the ER. Darcy wasn't there anymore. He double-checked with a nurse that she'd been taken into surgery.

Jackson found a seat and rested his head in his hands. He straightened and watched the people milling through the ER. Mostly doctors and nurses. He looked at each one a little closer, remembering that Chloe had worn a disguise to the press conference, so she wouldn't be above dressing like a medical professional to gain access to Darcy.

He settled deeper into his chair once he was confident none of the medical staff was Chloe. Gavin was right. Jackson had no solid evidence that Chloe was in the hospital. He knew, though, that letting his guard down was not an option.

He waited.

Twenty minutes later, the nurse he had talked to earlier came toward him. He burst to his feet. "How is she?"

"In addition to the cut to her stomach, the blow to her head was pretty severe. The doctors want to see if she wakes up on her own. We'll need to do a scan of her brain to assess if there is any permanent damage. The cut on her arm was superficial."

"I need to be with her. I'm a police officer and she's in a degree of danger of being attacked again."

The nurse's eyes grew wide, but she seemed to regain her composure. "I'll make sure the staff who will be taking care of her on the third floor knows that."

"Good, we're working on getting an officer posted outside her door. Until then, I'll stay in the room with her," Jackson said. "What room is she being taken to?"

"Three thirteen," the nurse replied.

Jackson jogged toward the elevators. He

pushed the button to call the elevator and waited for the car to arrive. Growing impatient and not wanting Darcy to be alone for even a few minutes, he glanced around for the stairs. The run would get rid of some of his nervous energy.

He sprinted up the stairs to the third floor. A nurse was just stepping out of Darcy's room when he arrived. Jackson explained the situation.

"I just took her vitals. Everything seems stable," the nurse said. "Does Miss Fields have any relatives?"

"Her sister, who's on an overnight field trip."

"You might want to give her a call just to let her know."

"I don't know the number and I think Darcy's phone is still back at the house."

"Maybe later then. In these kinds of situations, it's good to have family around." The nurse headed down the hall toward the nurses' station.

Jackson entered the room and scooted a chair closer to Darcy's bed. The nurse mentioning about family made Jackson remember that he hadn't locked up Darcy's apartment in his haste to follow the ambulance. He didn't know when her sister was due back.

He made a call into headquarters to request

an officer go to the apartment, search it, get Darcy's phone and make sure the place was locked up.

Jackson pushed up from his chair and leaned over Darcy. Even in the dim light, she looked cute. Her cheeks had a pink tinge to them. "Come back to me, Darcy." He brushed his thumb over her chin. "I miss you already."

Jackson sat back down in the silent dark room. His eyelids grew heavy with fatigue. At some point, he knew he'd have to go out to check on Smokey and let him out of the car for a while. He napped in short spurts, waking when a nurse came in to check on Darcy and when he heard hushed voices in the hallway.

His phone buzzed with a text from Lani Jameson that Darcy's apartment was locked up tight and that she'd arrange for the phone to be dropped off. He drifted off again and then woke some time later. The sound of Darcy's breathing was a comfort to him.

He checked to see if an officer was posted outside her room. Glad to see one there, Jackson left to check on Smokey. Even though she had protection, he didn't want to leave her at all.

Darcy awoke in total darkness. Fear gripped her heart. She had no idea where she was. She waited for her eyes to adjust to the light and to absorb the sensory information around her.

She had a moment of thinking Chloe had kidnapped her and was holding her hostage. The last thing she remembered was breaking free of Chloe's grasp. Even the memory of the attack caused her to take in an intense breath.

Her hand touched the cool metal of the railing that surrounded her bed. She could just discern the outline of an IV stand with a bag hanging from it. She was in a hospital. She turned her head one way and then the other.

An empty chair had been pushed very close to her bed. Someone had been in the room with her. Her sister? Or maybe Jackson?

Feet padded in the hallway then stopped. It sounded like someone was standing right outside her open door. A new wave of fear gripped her. When she turned her head to look, there was no one standing on the threshold. Her mind was playing tricks on her.

She listened to her heartbeat drumming in her ears. The window curtains were drawn. She had no idea what time it was or how long she'd been out. It must be late at night.

She heard more voices outside her door. One of them sounded familiar. Jackson was here in the hospital. She released a breath and rested her palm on her chest. Everything was going to be okay.

Jackson stood in the doorway. Light coming from the hallway revealed that his expression and even his posture changed when he saw her. He rushed over to her and gripped her hand. "Hey, you're awake."

"Barely," she said. "Did Chloe get away again?"

Jackson nodded. "Every officer is on high alert at this point. They don't think she'll leave the city with the trial so close and you still able to testify."

She touched her forehead where there was a bandage. "What happened?"

"You had a pretty big gash. The doctor will do a scan and wants to keep you until he's sure you are out of the woods. The cut into your stomach was pretty deep."

"Right now, I have a pounding headache." She rested her head on the pillow and touched her stomach. "And I think the pain pills are wearing off."

Jackson leaned over her, gazing into her eyes. Even in the dim light, he beamed affection and connection. "Sorry I wasn't here when you came to. I had to go out and walk Smokey."

"Thank you for staying with me."

"There's an officer posted outside your door. Unfortunately, I have to start my shift any minute."

She felt a tightening in her chest.

"Sarge extended me some grace because I wanted to make sure you were going to be okay." He reached for her hand and squeezed.

Releasing her hand, he sat in the chair that had been scooted close to her bed.

She stared at the ceiling. "What time is it?"

"Just a little past 2:00 a.m."

"I'm starving. Do you think they would bring me some food?"

He laughed. "It never hurts to try." He pushed the call button toward her hand.

She fumbled with the device, which was the size of a TV remote control, until it made a binging noise.

A woman in her early twenties stuck her head inside the room. "Hey, you're awake."

"Awake and starving. Is there any way I could get something to eat?" Darcy asked.

"The cafeteria is closed, but they might be able to bring up a sandwich."

"Anything would be fine with me," she said.

A few minutes later, a tray with two sandwiches and two juice boxes was brought in by a different woman. "The nurse suggested putting an extra serving on there in case your friend was hungry. Both of you have had quite a long night."

"Thanks," Jackson said, standing. He unwrapped the first sandwich while Darcy struggled into a sitting position. "Here, let me help you with that." He readjusted her pillow and then pushed the button that raised the top end of the bed.

His attentiveness touched her heart.

He grabbed the second sandwich and unwrapped it, handing it to Darcy.

She bit into the sandwich. Cold ham and cheese never tasted so good.

Jackson spoke between bites. "I got in touch with your sister. She'll come by as soon as she gets home from the field trip, and your phone is here."

"You took care of a lot while I was out of it."

While they ate, a uniformed officer stuck his head inside. "Just saying hi now that you're awake. I'm here to guard you, Miss Fields."

She smiled at him.

Jackson took the last bites of his sandwich in a hurry. He must be anxious to get to work, Darcy thought as she sipped at her orange juice.

Jackson answered his ringing phone. "I'm ready to go to work… Really… You think it might be her… Yes, count me in. I want to be there for the takedown… I can meet you there in twenty. Bring a uniform for me," he said, turning off his phone and rising from his chair.

"There's an athletic facility where the biathlon team trains," he told Darcy. "Someone who lives near the facility phoned in and said they thought they saw a person wandering around like they were looking for a way in. It could be Chloe. Three other K-9 officers are meeting me there." He touched her shoulder and then pointed to the door where the guard was partially visible. "You're in good hands."

He leaned over and kissed the uninjured side of her forehead. "Hopefully, the next time you see me, I'll have good news about Chloe's capture."

He stepped out of her room.

She felt like a balloon losing air when he was no longer close to her. The care he'd showed her made her want to be with him always. When he wasn't close, she could feel the chasm of loss. What was this feeling blossoming inside her? Maybe it was just because he had been so kind and attentive. She shook her head softly. There was something deeper going on.

Darcy lay back and closed her eyes. She prayed for Jackson's safety and for the rest of the team.

SIXTEEN

In the predawn hours, Jackson and the rest of the assigned team assembled near the athletic facility. Gavin, who was there to coordinate the search, had obtained a blueprint of the layout, which included a pool, weight room and running track, along with a rifle range. The team—Belle Montera, Tyler Walker, Jackson and their K-9 partners—had positioned itself a few blocks from the facility so the lights of their vehicles wouldn't draw attention if Chloe was hiding there.

They each agreed to search a separate quadrant and look for a point of entry where the "suspicious person," whom they believed to be Chloe Cleaves, might have broken in. Since the call had come in that the facility might have an intruder, a patrol officer had been dispatched to circle the facility. He had reported no sign of someone trying to enter or leave.

Gavin rolled up the blueprint. "Keep radio

communication to a minimum. Use flashlights only as necessary. If she is in there, we don't want to alert her to our presence. The tracker dog will work off the scent from the wig she left behind. Be safe. Let's go."

After putting on their night-vision goggles, they separated and hurried up the street. The buildings they ran past were all dark. The athletic facility was a two-story brick structure with an adjacent parking lot. The only car in the lot was the patrol officer's and he was still watching the place. That didn't mean Chloe hadn't found a way of escape out of view of the officer—if it was even her who had been spotted—or that she wasn't hiding somewhere inside just waiting for the officer to leave.

Heart pounding, Jackson circled the building with Smokey, moving slowly in the dark. He had a view of the pool through several large windows. From what he could see, everything looked quiet inside.

His radio beeped and Belle came on the line, speaking in a whisper. "I think we found the point of entry. Southside door is open. Looks like the lock has been jiggered."

Jackson circled the facility again, looking for signs of movement inside and outside. The windows on the part of the structure he had just passed were small and high up, likely the dressing rooms.

He found the open door that Belle had mentioned. Procedure dictated that they search their assigned quadrant even if it meant filtering through the open door. Once he entered, he didn't see any other member of the team.

"I'm in," he said into his radio.

As he moved through the facility to where he was supposed to search, he heard the other officers whisper a quiet "I'm in" over their radios, as well.

Jackson circled the swimming pool. The smell of chlorine was heady in the air. Above the pool, on the second floor, there was a viewing area with a railing—a sort of balcony that looked down on the pool.

He and Smokey cleared several of the rooms adjacent to pool, an equipment storage room and an office.

With Smokey taking the lead, Jackson returned to the main pool area. The night-vision goggles revealed other doors on the other side of the pool that he needed to check out. He looked once again at the viewing area above the pool.

His heart skipped a beat. A shadow danced on the back wall. Something or someone was moving around up there. He advised the team of where he was headed and circled the pool until he found the narrow stairway that led up to the viewing area.

Jackson took the stairs slowly, trying to be as quiet as possible. If Chloe was there, she would have seen him enter the pool area. He came to a door that was slightly ajar and pulled his weapon, Smokey perched beside him.

Easing the door open, he stepped inside and turned in a half circle to clear all four corners of the viewing area. The room contained some folding chairs positioned close to the railing that looked down on the pool. A couch and beanbag chair were positioned by the far wall. Some children's books and toys were stored in a box by the couch. There was a second door that led to a hallway.

He let out a heavy breath. Maybe he'd been wrong. He stepped toward the railing and gazed at the pool.

Static came across his radio and then he heard Tyler's voice. "I'm in the area where the rifles and ammunition are stored. The scent was really strong through here." There was a pause on the other end. "Looks like someone broke the glass and took a rifle. The lock on the ammunition drawer is disabled, as well."

Jackson froze in his tracks. Chloe was armed again. His first thought was that she wasn't even there anymore. She'd broken in to get the gun and ammo and could be across town by now, trying to get access to Darcy. Before they could draw that kind of a conclusion, they needed to clear the entire facility. He moved back down the stairs and worked his way over to the doors on the other side of the pool. He and Smokey entered the first locker room and checked the larger lockers, bathrooms and shower stalls. He stepped back out into the main area and hurried to the second locker room.

Smokey stiffened when they stood on the threshold. With his weapon drawn, Jackson entered slowly, working in his way past the benches and pulling back shower curtains. These lockers were too small for a person to hide in. Smokey still seemed agitated. The place was empty but maybe Chloe had been in there at some point.

The rest of the team had grown quiet. No mention of even having cleared a section of the facility. The silence was eerie. The thrumming of his heart in his ears augmented as he returned to the pool area.

Once again, he stared up at the observation balcony. If he was Chloe, he would hide there. It provided a view of much of the facility and of the people coming and going. The pool was at the center of the building. Most of the doors to other parts of facility connected to the pool, with the exception of the rifle range, which was separated by a long corridor.

Jackson circled the pool deck again, wondering if there was a second way to access the observation area, which would mean a way to escape. He remembered the second door. He returned to the balcony, stepped through the second door and out into the hallway. He followed it all the way to the end. There was another stairway down.

A door slammed somewhere not too far from his and Smokey's position. He hurried down the stairs, where he found Belle with her German shepherd, Justice. She looked not quite human in her goggles.

"Sorry," she whispered. "I was trying to shut the door quietly."

"Find anything?"

"Justice picked up a hint of a scent, nothing strong. Honestly, I think she came and got the gun and left. That's where the scent was a for-sure thing."

"With that patrol officer circling the facility, escape would be tricky. He would have seen her if she went out the door she broke in through. We know she was here at some point.

I'm not convinced she was able to leave. I'm doing one more sweep," Jackson said.

"Sarge hasn't called us off yet. I'm going take Justice down that hall and up to those second-floor offices. Leave no stone unturned, right?"

"Lots of places a person could hide in here. Might as well check every nook and cranny." Jackson headed back up the stairs to the observation deck that provided him with a bird's-eye view of much of the facility. He stared out the window, taking in each segment of the area around the pool.

He caught a flash of movement out of the corner of his eye. For a moment, he thought it was an officer who had traveled outside an assigned area because the K-9 had picked up on a scent. Whoever it was had slipped out of view through an open door.

If something had been found, why wasn't anyone on the radio?

"Davison, here. Has another officer slipped into my quadrant?"

Gavin answered back immediately. "Negative."

Another door, ten feet from the open one where he had seen movement, popped open. Jackson barely had time to register that he was seeing a rifle barrel aimed at him before the shot reverberated through the whole facility.

Pain sliced into his shoulder, causing his entire body to shudder. He leaned over the railing with a view of the water below. He reached for his radio.

The intensity of having been shot was like nothing he'd ever experienced. His vision blurred as he fumbled to make his fingers work the radio. He felt like he couldn't breathe, as though the air was being suctioned out of his lungs.

He clicked on his radio. His voice was whispy-weak. All he could manage to say was, "She's here. I'm shot."

Sarge's voice came across the line. "On my way."

Jackson looked up. Everything in front of him was wavy and out of focus. He thought he saw Chloe step out from behind the door and raise her rifle to take another shot at him. He doubled over in pain. He was a sitting duck up here.

The rest of the team had to be headed toward his quadrant. He was half hung over the railing, trying to move, to at least find the strength to lay flat on the floor and crawl backward. He could not will his body into motion.

His world started to go black. He had the

sensation of whirling through space. Had he been hit again? Was he losing consciousness? His vision narrowed right before he felt his body falling. He hit the water. Then he was gasping for air and flaying his arms and legs.

Dark brown sticks moved through the water toward him. They weren't sticks. It was his dog. Smokey had jumped in after him.

Jackson felt a tug on his back of his neck. Smokey was trying to pull him to the surface. It was a struggle to make his arm with the bullet wound work, but he kicked his legs. He felt himself being dragged. His head popped up above the surface. Gavin had jumped into the pool and was swimming toward him. He saw two other sets of legs—one K-9 and one human—at the edge of the pool.

He felt himself being half carried, half dragged and then being stretched out on the tile surrounding the pool.

Smokey licked his forehead.

"Did you get her?" he asked.

Gavin put his face very close to Jackson's, water dripping off his hair onto Jackson's face. "Tyler and Dusty are after her."

"You have to get her." Pain surged through Jackson's body. He groaned.

Gavin's expression changed and he spoke to

Belle. "That ambulance is on its way, right?"
He sounded upset.

"Yes, sir."

Jackson could barely get the words out. "The
bullet wound. How bad?"

Gavin stared at his shoulder for a second.
"No major organs. Tore through quite a bit of
flesh."

Jackson put his head down on the cold tile.
Everything seemed to be whirling around him.
The only thing that was real was his dog lying
beside him and licking his cheek.

"You have to catch Chloe. For Darcy's sake."
Jackson wasn't sure if he had spoken the words
or just thought them.

The pain was unbearable.

Darcy was sitting up in bed when a nurse
pushing a wheelchair and wearing a very serious expression came into the room. The police
officer who had been standing outside Darcy's
door was right behind her.

"What's going on?"

"A decision has been made to move you to a
room with no windows," the nurse said.

The officer stepped forward. "I'll be escorting you."

"What's happened? What's going on?" Her
mind reeled. Jackson and the other officers

must not have been able to catch Chloe. "Let me guess. Chloe is out there and she's armed. They think she might try to shoot me through the window."

The patrol officer looked at the nurse and then at Darcy. "It's just a precaution."

"They wouldn't be moving me unless they thought I was in even more danger."

The nurse pushed the wheelchair toward her. "You haven't been out of that bed since you were brought in. If you feel at all dizzy, we can move you in the chair."

"I'd like to try to walk."

The nurse pushed the bedside rail down out of the way. "Take it slow. Swing your legs off the side of the bed first."

As she sat with her legs dangling, Darcy still felt light-headed. The nurse held out a hand for support.

"Walking will be good for you at this point, but if you feel at all unstable, let me know."

Dragging her IV with her, Darcy took a few hesitant steps. "I walk like an old lady." They worked their way slowly out into the hall. Fear overtook her as she stared at all the people bustling around.

Chloe was still out there. Chloe wanted her dead. If she couldn't shoot Darcy from a distance, she'd find another way. Darcy hadn't been willing to admit it until now, but the attack in her apartment had traumatized her in a deep way, more so than the others. She had seen the intensity of Chloe's rage up close.

The nurse held Darcy's arm while the officer walked on the other side of her, pushing the wheelchair. She was in good hands, but that didn't mean Chloe wouldn't make an appearance.

The officer cleared his throat. "You should probably know that your friend who sat with you, Officer Davison, was brought in a few hours ago."

Darcy stopped and stared up at the police officer. "What happened?"

"A gunshot wound," the nurse said.

"Some of Chloe Cleaves' handiwork, unfortunately," the officer admitted. "He's in surgery right now. The bullet didn't hit any vital organs, but it tore his shoulder up."

Maybe it was just panic over what might happen to Jackson, but the news gave her strength and energy. "I don't want to go to my room. I want to sit with the K-9 officers. I'm sure some of them are standing by."

"You're still very weak." The nurse looked up at the officer.

"I insist," Darcy said. "I'm not going to lie in a bed alone when Jackson might be fighting for his life. He has been there for me through everything."

The officer shrugged. "No safer place for her to be than surrounded by police officers. I'll stay with her, no matter what."

"I suppose it would be better for you to be sitting up and maybe moving around a little. I'll have to clear it with the doctor. I'll come to get you if he doesn't give the okay."

They led Darcy to the waiting room outside the surgery wing. Officers Belle Montera and Lani Jameson were there. Belle stood when Darcy came into the room. She walked over to Darcy and grasped her hands. "Good to see you. Jackson has been in surgery for about an hour now. Gavin had to get back to headquarters, so Lani came over." Belle nodded at the tall blonde.

"Chloe is still on the run. The whole K-9 Unit has been praying for a good outcome for Jackson and getting Chloe back into custody," Lani told her.

Belle led her to a seat and Darcy lowered herself slowly into the chair. Feeling a sharp pain through her stomach where she'd been stabbed, a light patina of sweat appeared on her forehead from the effort of moving around. The news that Chloe had not been captured didn't sit well with her.

Belle patted her hand. "I know it will mean so much to Jackson that you came here to support him. His family in Texas has been notified. He doesn't have any family close by, except for Smokey, and they won't allow him into the waiting room."

"I think you guys are his family."

"And you, too. He talks about you a lot," Lani said.

"He and Smokey are a big part of my life, too," Darcy said. *I'm starting to wish he could be an even bigger part*, she thought. "Is one of the other officers looking out for Smokey?"

"Yes, Tyler will watch him until Jackson is strong enough to care for him."

Darcy felt herself growing weak as they waited for close to three quarters of an hour. Belle got her some hot coffee and a bag of chips from the vending machine. Moving around had taken a lot out of her. She probably should be lying down in her bed, but she didn't want to miss any news about Jackson or lose out on an opportunity to see him once he was out of surgery. He had been strong for her, so she would be strong for him.

Darcy sipped her coffee and waited with Belle, Lani and her personal protection officer.

A man dressed in surgical scrubs emerged

from a hallway and walked toward them. They all stood.

"He's been out of surgery for about half an hour and he's awake. I didn't want to alert you until he was stabilized. He can have one visitor at a time. If he starts to fatigue, we need to leave him so he can fully recover." The surgeon turned toward Darcy. "Are you Darcy?"

She nodded.

"He's been asking for you," he said.

"You should go see him first then," Belle said as she cupped a hand on Darcy's shoulder.

The surgeon left and the officer escorted Darcy down the hall to the recovery room. It made her feel good to know that with no family close by, she was the first person Jackson had wanted to see.

"I'll just be right outside the door," the officer said.

"Thanks."

Darcy stepped into the room. The paleness of Jackson's expression and the way his skin seemed to hang on his face sent a shockwave through her.

"Hey, don't look so glum." Jackson gave her his trademark wink.

"She got to you." Darcy moved to the side of his bed and leaned in close to him. Even his eyes had lost their brightness.

Jackson grabbed her hand. "It's going to be okay."

Tears flowed as she squeezed his hand tighter. "I hate seeing you like this."

"Just part of the job," he said.

She wiped at her eyes. "I'm sorry. I think I have finally reached my breaking point."

"Don't worry about the tears. You're a strong lady, Darcy. Anyone else would have fallen apart way sooner."

She met his eyes, seeing deep affection in his gaze. "So what did the doctors say about your injury?"

"The bullet tore up a lot of tissue. The damaged shoulder is not connected to my shooting hand, but I will probably be out of commission for a while. If I can work at all, I'll probably be on light duty or behind a desk."

The news upset her. Jackson was in his element when he was working with Smokey and the other K-9 officers. "I'm sure that won't be easy. We have both been forced to take a vacation neither of us wanted."

His expression grew serious. "Did you hear from anyone? Did they get Chloe?"

Darcy hated giving him the news that his valiant effort had all been for nothing. She shook her head. "I'm so sorry," she said.

The disappointment in his features was intense.

She took a seat in the bedside chair, and they visited a while longer until Jackson started to nod off. She felt quite fatigued herself. She pushed herself to her feet but held on to the back of the chair for support. "I'll come by later in the day, after you've had a good sleep."

Though she could tell he was struggling to keep his eyes open, he managed another wink. "Or maybe I'll come by and see you since I'm in the neighborhood."

"I'm sure we'll work something out."

She made her way out of his room. The officer was waiting for her in the hallway. All the movement had made her rather achy and she was now kind of wishing for the wheelchair...

She was escorted to her new windowless room and, with some help from the nurse, got into her bed. She winced, the pain from her stomach wound intensifying.

"Still feeling some pain?" the nurse asked.

She nodded. "I think I overdid it."

"We can get you some more pain medication."

Darcy nodded again, struggling to stay awake. "I'm glad I got up and moved around."

The nurse left and returned with pain medication and a pill to help her sleep.

Darcy slept, barely waking when the nurses

came in to check her vitals, after which she fell into an even deeper sleep.

The next time she stirred, the room was dark, as was the hallway. A different officer was probably on duty outside her door by now. Someone was moving around in her room. She recognized a nurse's uniform, though she wasn't sure what the nurse was doing on the other side of the room so close to the bathroom.

Her eyelids were heavy as the nurse fussed around her bedside and then switched out the IV bag. Darcy was having a hard time putting her thoughts together. The sleep medication hadn't worn off yet. She had no idea how long she'd been sleeping, and she didn't have the strength to turn to check the clock on her bedside table.

She closed her eyes as the fog of fatigue overtook her.

She heard the nurse's shoes pad softly out the door. She listened to the drip of the IV, feeling a stinging sensation at the point where the fluid entered her body.

Darcy's eyes shot open. She grabbed the IV tube and squeezed it so no more of the fluid could reach her body. It had taken her a second to process what had been off about the nurse who had been in her room. The IV bag she had discarded had still been full.

Maybe it was just her imagination, but Darcy thought she could feel the little bit of poison that had gotten into her burning her veins. A sweat broke out on her forehead. Her heart raced.

She couldn't reach her call button without letting go of the IV.

She cried out. "Somebody, help me! Please!" Though she feared that it would be Chloe who would return to her room.

A female officer stuck her head inside the room. "Is everything okay?"

"Use my call button to get medical staff in here. I'm pretty sure there's poison in this IV." Darcy fought off the dizziness. "I think some of it got into me. Chloe Cleaves was in my room. You need to find her before she gets away."

"My instructions are to stay with you at all times."

"Make an exception and see if you can get a search for her started. I don't know if there are other officers in the building or what."

"I'll go as soon as the medical staff gets here," the policewoman told her.

That seemed like the wisest thing in case Chloe was waiting around to make sure her handiwork had been successful.

The officer said "Did you see her? Do you know for sure it was Chloe?"

Darcy had no idea what Chloe had put in the IV, but her heart was beating erratically. Was that just panic or was the poison something that would make her heart explode? Talking cohesively took some effort. "I never saw her face. I was half asleep. But she was acting weird. She didn't take my vitals. She was standing over by the bathroom. The IV bag she discarded was still full."

"That does sound suspicious," the policewoman agreed.

The officer waited until a nurse and then a doctor entered, which took less than a minute.

The doctor looked at Darcy. "What's going on here?"

Darcy let out a breath but could not form the words. She felt like she was shutting down. Her fear escalated. How much poison had gotten into her?

The female officer answered for her. "She thinks she might have been poisoned through that IV."

Darcy had a hard time focusing as the doctor leaned in and disconnected the IV.

"I don't want to take any chances. Let's flush her system," the doctor said to the nurse. "Take a blood sample to find out what's in that

IV. See if we can figure out what is going on. Let's get this done. Stat."

Still feeling like her brain was in ether, Darcy turned her head to where the woman she was pretty sure was Chloe had been. A chair with a plastic bag containing Darcy's personal items had been pushed close to the bathroom. Her thoughts became foggy as she wondered if Chloe had taken something out of her bag.

SEVENTEEN

Jackson sat up in the hospital bed. He was bored out of his mind. Through the window, he saw that it was dark outside. He had slept through most of the day and into the night. Sitting still didn't agree with him, let alone just lying in bed. He wanted to be moving, to be doing something, and he missed Smokey. He swung his legs over the side of the bed and stepped onto the floor with care. The painkillers were still working. His shoulder felt stiff and sore, but it wasn't screaming with pain.

He walked over to the bag containing his personal items and pulled out his phone.

The only people he knew who would be up at this hour would be on-duty K-9 officers and he didn't want to distract them while they were on the job.

There was a text message from Darcy. Just the sight of her name and number made him smile.

When you feel up to it, can we meet to talk? There is a place on the fourth floor that is super quiet.

He typed in his reply.

Hi, Darcy. I'm up and could use some company.

Her reply was almost immediate. She must be as bored as he was.

Great. Fourth floor lounge, west wing. See you in ten minutes.

He had no idea where the west wing was, but it would be easy enough to find out. Taking his phone with him, he walked out into the hallway, which was quiet. He saw no sign of a nurses' or administrative station, but he did find an unoccupied waiting area that had a map of the hospital. The west wing was down a floor from where he was on the fifth floor.

As he made his way to the elevator, he passed a janitor mopping the floor, a woman in hospital gown sitting by a window, and a woman carrying a clipboard, whom he presumed to be a doctor. Other than that, he didn't see any other people.

He pressed the elevator button and stepped inside when the car arrived, getting off on the floor below his. Darcy, he recalled, was on the third floor; she must have figured this would be a good in-between place to meet.

Once he was on the fourth floor, he encountered a nurses' station with only one nurse bent over a keyboard and focused on her work. As he walked past, she didn't even look up to acknowledge him.

The earbuds she wore probably shut out most of the sound or maybe she was transcribing something. She had a sort of dashboard in front of her where, he assumed, lights would flash when a patient pressed a call button. He ambled past numerous rooms where the people inside, hooked to machines, lay nearly lifeless in their beds. This must be an ICU floor, he thought to himself.

He kept walking until he found a sign that informed him he was in the west wing. He entered a large lounge area, noting the circular setup of three different couch arrangements. Large floor-to-ceiling windows looked out on both sides of the city. The place was completely empty.

The hall beyond the lounge was completely dark. It must be a part of the hospital that wasn't used.

He turned a half circle and pulled out his phone.

Where are you?

On my way. I move slow.

The walk had tired him out. He sat in a lounge chair and stared out the large window at the city lights. Just across the street was another high-rise building that was part of the hospital.

He stared down at his phone as his heartbeat kicked up a notch.

This was a setup. Darcy was not on her way.

He dove to the ground just as glass shattered around him. Pain shot through his wounded shoulder as he tried to drag himself across the floor to seek cover behind a couch, an almost impossible task with his bad shoulder. Another shot was fired. He pressed even lower into the floor.

He doubted the nurse who was way down the hall and wearing earbuds would respond. As far as he knew, no one on the floor could get out of bed.

He wasn't going to get anywhere trying to drag himself soldier-style. Instead he rolled toward a chair that would provide some cover. Though he tried to protect his shoulder, the move caused pain that radiated through his whole body. With some effort, he tucked himself up behind the chair, realizing he'd dropped his phone in the effort to save himself. To try to retrieve it would make him an easy target. It was a long stretch where he'd be out in the open before he could get to the safety of the hallway. Because of his injury, crawling was out of the question. He'd have to stand and run.

Jackson angled his body and craned his neck so he had a view of the building not more than the width of a street away. The building where Chloe was probably lying on her stomach, looking through the scope of her rifle, and waiting for the chance to take him out.

She must have gotten Darcy's phone.

That realization sent a new wave of fear through him. What if Chloe had done Darcy in and now was coming back to finish him off? He had to get to that nurses' station. He bolted to his feet and ran at an angle toward the hallway. Gripping his shoulder where the pain had intensified, he bent forward and kept running. He sprinted past the hospital rooms where people lay unconscious.

He was doubled over by the time he made it to the nurses' station. The nurse stood and pulled out her earbuds, running to him just as he collapsed on the floor.

Darcy pulled the covers up to her neck and stared at the ceiling. It had been hours since the medical staff had flushed the poison from her body and still she couldn't sleep. All the trauma to her body had made her sleep through most of the day and there'd been no word on whether they had tracked down Chloe.

The female officer was still outside her door, so Darcy took in several deep breaths and prayed, trying to calm down.

A nurse entered her room. "Still awake, huh?"

Darcy nodded her head.

"The doctor had a preliminary test done on the IV solution. It seemed it contained a lethal amount of digitalis."

"Heart medication," Darcy said.

"So, you were right."

The nurse took Darcy's vitals and had just turned to leave when Darcy called out to her. "Can you get me my phone? It's over in that plastic bag."

"Sure, no problem."

Darcy doubted anyone would be up at this hour, but she could send some texts to her sister, to Harlan and, of course, to Jackson if he hadn't heard the news already.

The nurse pulled out the watch Darcy had been wearing when she was admitted to the hospital. She searched the bag. "Mind if I dump this out? I can't seem to find your phone."

"Go ahead," Darcy said. "I know it was in there. Jackson had it delivered from my apartment."

The nurse spilled the contents of the bag onto the rolling table by Darcy's bed. No phone.

Fear gripped her.

"Chloe must have taken it." Why? Chloe must of have left the room assuming that the poison would kill Darcy. Her stomach tightened. Chloe had made it clear she wanted Jackson dead, too. "I have a friend staying in the hospital. Jackson Davison. Could you check on his status for me?"

The nurse, who had been picking up Darcy's personal items, slowed in her action. "We didn't want to worry you. There was another attempt on his life a short time ago. He was on the fourth floor. Someone shot at him through the window."

"Is he okay?"

"Relatively. He never should have been out of bed in his condition so soon after being shot in the first place. He wore himself out."

"Did they catch the person who shot at him?" She knew it had to have been Chloe and that Chloe must have somehow lured Jackson to the fourth floor with her phone.

"I don't know. If I hear any news, I will let you know."

"Look, I can't sleep. Can the officer on duty wheel me down to his room? Even if he's still sleeping. Can I just hang out until he wakes up?"

"I'll see what I can do," the nurse said. "I was on duty earlier when he asked to see you. You two seem very close. It must be true love."

"We're friends. Good friends. That's all." Even as she spoke, Darcy knew that wasn't true anymore. What was between them ran way deeper than that.

The nurse left the room.

Darcy rested her head on the pillow and waited for the nurse to return.

Within minutes, the female police officer entered her room, pushing a wheelchair. "Heard you wanted to go for a ride."

The officer helped her out of bed and wheeled her down the hall and into the elevator.

When they entered Jackson's room, he was wide awake and sitting up.

"Guess we both had a little excitement." Darcy said as the policewoman left to wait outside the door.

"Yeah, I heard. I'm glad you're here." He lifted his hand, showing that he was holding his phone. "They recovered my phone, but not yours. They thought they might be able to track Chloe by your phone. She may have ditched it. The doctors won't let me do anything but rest, which is making me nuts."

"Sometimes, doctors have good advice." Darcy pushed the wheelchair closer to his bed. "You look more worn out than me."

"I have been on the phone. NYPD has a ton of officers combing the building where Chloe probably set up shop to take aim at me."

"But they haven't found her yet?"

He shook his head.

"She might be dressed as a nurse."

"When they told me what had happened to you, I thought that might be the case. How else could she have gotten past that officer?" Jackson placed his head back on the pillow. "I know they didn't tell me sooner about you being poisoned because I needed to rest, but I wish I had known."

"Maybe you should try to get some sleep."

He smiled. "You're not sleeping, either."

A silence fell between them and Darcy remembered what the nurse had said. *It must be true love.* What she realized was that if she had used discernment about the character of the detective who had only showed her affection to move his case along, she would not have been hurt. It wasn't about not dating cops. It was about seeing the heart of the person in front of her. Darcy knew now that Jackson had shown over and over that he was a man of integrity. The right time to talk about how her feelings for him had changed never seemed to happen. If she was honest with herself, bringing up the subject made her afraid. Everything he'd said in the past indicated he wasn't over his last breakup. Her affection for him ran so deep, she wasn't sure if their friendship could survive a rebuff from him. She didn't want to risk the friendship by asking for something more.

When Jackson was ready, he would have to be the one to open that door. She couldn't bear the thought of his rejection.

"Some deep thoughts going on in that genius brain of yours," he said.

She shook her head. "Just pondering."

In the hallway, a familiar tune started to play. All the air left her lungs. She knew that melody. It was the ringtone for her phone.

She stood, still feeling a little wobbly.

Jackson sat straighter in his bed. "Darcy, what is it?"

The phone stopped ringing.

When she stepped out into the hall, the female officer assigned to protect her was standing by a medical cart, holding a phone.

"Someone left their phone on the cart."

"That's my ringtone. May I see it?" She held out her hand. There were probably other people in the world who chose old hymns as ringtones. Even before the officer handed it over, Darcy knew it was her phone. The glittery cover was hers.

"Did you see anyone by that cart who might have left it?"

"There was a lot of traffic through here a minute ago," the officer said. "Some kind of emergency up the hall. The cart has been there for at least twenty minutes."

Jackson stood in the doorway. "Darcy, what is it?"

"I think Chloe was here either twenty minutes ago and she left my phone on the cart or she swept through with a crowd of people a minute ago and left it."

Jackson still held his phone. "I'll let the other officers know. Some of them are still searching the hospital. If it was a few minutes ago, she might still be in the area."

"She's probably dressed as a nurse." Darcy stared down at the phone. She had five new texts. She clicked on the message icon. All five texts were from the same number and they all said the same thing.

You will not live to testify at Reuben's trial.

EIGHTEEN

Jackson paced the floor of the house where he and Darcy had stayed under protective custody since being released from the hospital three days ago. The trial was in two hours.

The house belonged to a retired police chief and his wife who'd gone south for the winter. A rotation of patrol and K-9 officers had been assigned to watch over him and Darcy.

As he paced, Smokey thudded his tail and licked his jaw. His way of asking if everything was okay.

"I'm just real nervous," said Jackson. He glanced at his police utility belt resting on the table. He was dressed in full uniform. Still not cleared for field duty, he had talked Gavin into letting him be one of the officers that escorted Darcy to and from the trial. Though he had healed a great deal, his shoulder still hurt when he tried to raise his arm up high.

Darcy entered the room. She wore jeans and

a baggy sweater. "Aren't you getting ready a little early?" she asked.

"I just feel like I need to do something."

She stared down at her clothes. "I guess I have the opposite response. I want to pretend like is not happening until the last minute."

He walked over to her and took her hands in his. "All of the NYPD has taken every measure to ensure your safety. Since Chloe's favorite thing is to shoot from a distance, officers are watching the tall buildings surrounding the courthouse. And no one will get into or out of those buildings without having to go past at least three officers and a metal detector."

She looked up into his eyes. "I know that they will do everything to keep me safe. And I know that once I testify, the question about me being able to do my job will go away." She glanced to the side at a window with its curtains drawn, as it had been since they'd both been brought here. Her lip quivered. "But it doesn't mean Chloe will leave me alone. I'm sure she will want revenge for Reuben being put away for good."

Jackson cupped her arm just below the shoulder. "If Chloe shows up for that trial, which we believe she will, we have taken every measure to ensure her capture."

He did not want to tell Darcy that they

couldn't guard every inch of the route that led to the courthouse. They had chosen a route that was not predictable, but there were only so many ways to get to the courthouse. If Chloe had figured out where they were hiding, she would have attacked by now. They both had received threatening texts. Always from a throwaway phone. The texts made it clear that Chloe wanted both of them dead.

"I can put some coffee on for us if you like," Darcy offered. "And I think there are still some leftovers of that casserole Lani brought when she came on duty."

"Food sounds good. I don't think coffee would help me calm down."

She laughed and retreated into the kitchen. He followed her. Smokey waited until he was given the command to follow, as well.

He watched as Darcy pulled down, plated and heated up the casserole in the microwave. Even under these trying circumstances, he had enjoyed his time with Darcy. The curtains had remained drawn and neither of them had stepped outside since they had taken up residence.

The officer standing guard was also the one to stay with Smokey when he went out in the yard.

The days had been spent praying together,

playing board games or sitting together on the couch, each of them reading their respective books. Even with the shadow of danger that had hung over each day, Jackson relished their time together. These days had made him realize that he could picture them having a life together of being more than just friends.

She set a steaming plate of lasagna on the table where he was seated. "Why are you looking at me like that?"

He shook his head. "Just thinking."

She dished up some of the leftovers for herself and sat opposite him. "Just thinking about what?"

He shrugged. Now was not the time to broach the subject. They needed to get through the trial and the K-9 Unit needed to make sure Chloe was brought into custody.

He knew that one way or another, Chloe would make a last-ditch effort to get at Darcy before the trial. The text had made it clear that Chloe was out for revenge. After the trial, she might become a lot dodgier, laying low for months and then going after Darcy or him.

They had to catch her today.

Darcy finished her meal and went upstairs to shower and dress. The plan was to arrive an hour before the trial and enter the courthouse by a back door, though the amount of police they had surrounding her would call attention to her if anybody was watching.

Half an hour later, she met Jackson and Smokey downstairs. Belle Montera was waiting outside in the yard with Justice, who was trained for protection. Darcy pulled back the living-room curtain a few inches for a limited view of the street. There was a dark-colored SUV parked at the curb.

Jackson stepped toward her. "We'll be traveling in an umarked police car."

"That must be it out there right now." Her chest squeezed a little tighter.

He held out his arms and she fell into his embrace.

"I want to say that it's going to be okay. But I know that's not true. Not until we catch her," Jackson said.

Closing her eyes, Darcy relished the safety of his arms around her. "Thank you for being honest. You know I would have seen past you trying to paint a rosy picture."

He drew her closer, hugging her tight and then letting her go. "Let's do this. I'll go let Belle know we're ready. We'll walk out together. She and Justice will be behind us in a different car, also unmarked. We don't want to call attention in any way." Jackson left the room and opened the front door to call out to Belle.

Darcy took a deep breath, as though she were about to dive under water. Jackson returned, Belle and Justice right behind him. He commanded Smokey to fall in. "Let Smokey and I take the front." He looked over at Belle. "You and Justice can be behind Darcy until you have to get in your own car."

"Ready when you are," Belle said.

They walked out to the black SUV where a driver, another police officer, sat behind the wheel.

"I'll be up front. Smokey will ride in the back with you," Jackson told Darcy.

There was a comfort in knowing that the dog would be so close. He was a true protector.

Jackson opened the back door.

She caught a glimpse of Belle loading Justice into the vehicle that was parked about a block away before she got into the SUV. The windows of the SUV were tinted so no one could see her sitting inside.

Every precaution had been taken to ensure her safety. Why, then, did she still feel so afraid?

Jackson waited for Darcy to settle in the back seat and for Smokey to jump in beside her. He did a quick survey of his surroundings, glancing in his side mirror at Belle, who had her motor running and was waiting to pull away from the curb and slip in behind them.

There was no reason to think that Chloe knew where they'd been staying. Yet she'd been so clever about getting to both him and Darcy in the past, he knew he couldn't let his guard down.

He got in on the passenger side of the front seat.

"We're ready," he said.

Jackson had a feeling the drive through the city to the courthouse was going to be one of the longest of his life. The driver turned his wheel and pressed the gas, pulling out onto the street.

As the city whizzed by, Jackson found himself scanning the bridges and buildings and other high places a shooter might be waiting.

Traffic intensified around the courthouse. They took a side street that would lead to the back entrance. He noted that the number of news vans was triple what it usually was for a trial.

Darcy leaned toward Jackson, gripping the back of his seat. "That's her. I saw her."

Jackson scanned where Darcy had just pointed, seeing only an ocean of faces. It might be that Darcy was just on edge, but they couldn't take any chances. Jackson radioed to the K-9 officers who were standing by outside the courthouse, giving the street name and approximate location Darcy had said she'd seen Chloe.

Darcy looked down at the floor of the car. "She was there and then she faded back into the crowd. I know she can't see me in here… but still."

They were forced to double park in the parking lot behind the courthouse. Belle radioed that she had gotten stuck behind a truck in traffic that was at a standstill. Their driver couldn't leave the vehicle. Jackson and Smokey would be escorting Darcy into the courthouse alone.

"Stay in the vehicle until I am out and can open the door for you," Jackson said. He pushed open his door, glancing in every direction. There were several news vans parked a block away.

He opened the back door. Smokey jumped down on command. "We better hurry," he said, reaching in for Darcy. When he glanced over his shoulder, he saw one of the news crews racing toward them, followed by another two.

He wrapped his arms around Darcy. Smokey took up a position on the other side of her. The reporters clamored behind them, getting closer as they hurried to the courthouse rear entrance. Jackson reached out for the door and Darcy stepped inside. Jackson stayed between her and the approaching reporters until the door closed.

They stood in a long silent corridor.

"I have no idea how to get to the courtroom from here. I always go in the front or side entrance," said Darcy.

Jackson looked one way and then the other. "It can't be that hard. Let's go this way. I'm sure we'll see some signs or something familiar soon enough."

He pressed the button on his radio. They had positioned two other officers and their K-9s inside the courthouse. "Tyler, we've entered the back of the courthouse. I'm alone with Darcy. Can you tell me your position?"

"Waiting for you in the hallway just outside courtroom 203. There is a room off to the side of the courtroom where Darcy can wait until it's her turn to testify. We've made sure it's secure."

"We're on our way." Jackson signed off.

They worked their way through the labyrinth of the courthouse hallways, going up a set of stairs and following the signs that directed them down lengthy corridors. They encountered more people the closer they got to courtroom 203.

Jackson read numbers on the doors once they were in the right hallway. It wasn't hard to guess where Reuben's trial was to be held. At the end of the hall there was a cluster of police, reporters and curious citizens.

Darcy stopped when she saw the crowd. Several reporters spotted them and began to move in their direction. Tyler Walker stepped into their path along with Dusty. The intimidation factor of the K-9 was effective in stopping the reporters.

Tyler hurried over to Jackson and Darcy. "This way." He pointed down a hallway and led them into a room with no windows. Two couches faced each other on opposite walls. Darcy took a seat on one and Jackson sat beside her. Smokey rested at Jackson's feet.

"We'll be right outside this door." Tyler pointed to the door that led to the hallway they had just exited.

Darcy knew from having testified before that the door on the opposite side of the room lead to the courtroom.

She tilted her head toward the ceiling. "I wonder how long it's going to be."

Jackson rested his hand on hers. "Not sure."

"They must not have caught or even seen

Chloe. It would have come across your radio, right?"

"Probably, yes."

She stood and paced. "I know I saw her in that crowd. I'm not making it up."

"I believe you."

"What if she's in the courtroom?"

"The dogs will alert to her scent. Everyone watching the trial was screened before they were seated." Though she was putting up a good front, Jackson could tell she was afraid. He held out his arms. "You want a hug?"

She fell into his embrace. He held her tight.

A moment later, there was a knock on the door and the bailiff stuck his head inside the room. "Miss Fields, they are ready for you now."

Darcy glanced at Jackson and then petted Smokey.

Jackson could not go with her into the courtroom. "I'll see you in there in just a few minutes. And then I'll come back here when you're done."

She nodded. The bailiff opened the door and waited.

Once the door closed, Jackson commanded Smokey to fall in and they headed down into the courtroom where the public was allowed to enter. Jackson had to show his badge and squeeze through a substantial crowd outside the courtroom. By the time he was at the back of the room, Darcy had taken the stand and been sworn in. Jackson could only see the back of Reuben Bray's head. He didn't have to see the guy's face to know that he was probably smirking.

Darcy glanced at Reuben. Though she was trying not to show emotion, Jackson could tell that seeing him had shaken her.

Be strong, Darcy.

The prosecutor stepped toward her. "Miss Fields, would you please explain your qualifications as an expert witness?"

Darcy recited her qualifications and then answered a set of questions specific to the evidence that had led to Reuben's arrest and incarceration. Her answers were precise and to the point. Her voice exuded a natural confidence when she spoke about her work.

Jackson glanced over at one of the reporters. The woman, who had been so accusatory at a previous press conference, now wore an expression that suggested she was in a state of shock. As they had hoped, Darcy's professionalism would put an end to all the lies leveled at her and the Brooklyn K-9 Unit.

It was pretty clear to Jackson that Reuben

was going to jail for a long time based on Darcy's expert testimony.

He took in a deep breath for the first time in a long time.

A boom and a rush of wind surrounded Jackson. He felt his body being lifted up and thrown back down. Plaster and rubble rained down on top of him. Shoes scrambled all around him as chaos in the wake of the bomb blast broke out.

He could see people screaming but not hear them. The blast had caused temporary deafness. He stumbled to his feet. Smokey licked his hand. The dog was covered in dust and plaster, but appeared okay. He saw only one fellow officer hunched over but conscious. Jackson's attention was drawn to the front of the room. Darcy was no longer on the witness stand.

The panicked crowd was working its way out into the hallway. When he turned to look in that direction, a portion of the wall by the door was missing. The bomb may have just been placed outside the door. Maybe Chloe had gotten a grunt to do it for her. The explosion hadn't been strong enough to destroy the entire courtroom, just to create a distraction. Maybe so Chloe could get access to Darcy. In the confusion, she would have been able to sneak in.

The bomb had to have been dropped outside the door only minutes before it went off. The K-9 team had taken every precaution. So he had to assume that Cody, the bomb detection beagle, and his partner Detective Henry Roarke had been through the courtroom and surrounding area before the trial began.

Working his way toward the witness stand was like swimming upstream through the escaping crowd. He didn't see Reuben or his attorney. Maybe they had fled for the doors, as well.

Jackson didn't see Darcy anywhere. The bailiff was gone, as well. Maybe he had escorted her back to the waiting room. He found the door where witnesses entered.

A lady in a suit grabbed his arm. Her lips were moving but he couldn't hear her. He shook his head and pointed to his ears.

He opened the door and headed down the hallway. There were several doors where witnesses must wait to take the stand. When he checked the rooms, only one was occupied with an older man in a suit, probably someone who had been a victim of Reuben's theft. The man rose, indicating that he thought Jackson must have come to take him to testify. Jackson shook his head and gave a hand signal that the man should remain where he was.

With his hearing out of order, Jackson couldn't use his radio. He stepped out into the hallway, searching every face. People were crouched over and covered in dust and plaster. He feared the worst for Darcy.

He pushed through the crowd. Smokey remained close to him. The back of a blond woman's head caught his attention. The hair looked too shiny and perfect to be real. Chloe had brown hair, but she'd worn a disguise before at the press conference.

The woman was swallowed up by the crowd of panicked people. Jackson pressed forward. He spotted the back of the blond head again only farther away. This time he saw that the woman had her arm around another much shorter blonde. His heart skipped a beat. Darcy.

He lost sight of them again. He searched the faces of the people around him, hoping to enlist a fellow officer to help him capture Chloe and ensure Darcy was kept alive. He saw no other officers close by. True to their sense of duty, they must have all rushed toward where the bomb had gone off to help.

Jackson squeezed past people, praying that he would get to Darcy on time.

NINETEEN

Chloe held Darcy tightly around the waist. As the taller woman dragged her through the crowd, Darcy feared her stomach would end up bruised. Chloe seemed to know where her knife wound had been. She pressed her fingers against it, causing pain any time Darcy tried to twist free of her intense grip. Chloe was very strong. Any attempt to get away from her would be thwarted. The people around them were in such a panic over the bomb blast that there was no way she could get their attention. She didn't see any police officers close by.

Chloe guided her through the side door of the building. Darcy had a momentary view of the pandemonium on the wide front steps of the courthouse, but they were too far away for her to attract anyone's attention. Reporters, who had been watching the trial from news vans, were trying to get inside while people affected by the bomb blast pushed to get down the stairs.

Darcy tried to look over her shoulder. Again, Chloe pressed into her stomach. Pain shot through Darcy's body. She'd seen Jackson and Smokey at the back of the courtroom when she'd begun her testimony. Where were they now?

Outside at the front of the courthouse even more police officers and other first responders were arriving. The area surrounding the building was a sea of flashing lights.

Darcy had no doubt that Chloe's intention was to kill her, but knew she wasn't about to do it within the sight of law enforcement and risk getting caught. Chloe pulled her away from the crowd and down a side street, probably dragging her to a secluded spot so she could kill her and escape.

Darcy knew that. The crowd thinned. She had to get away. Chloe pushed her down an alley. Though she could still here the panic of the crowd, there was no one in the alley. Chloe dragged her toward a Dumpster. She swept her hand over the top of the closed container, grabbing a knife she must have stashed there earlier. In the three days they'd waited for the trial, Chloe had had time to scout the area around the courthouse and carefully plan.

Behind her, a dog barked. Chloe whirled her around as she pressed the knife into Darcy's throat. The dog was Smokey—but where was Jackson? The K-9 drew closer, continuing to bark in a threatening manner. When he was within a few feet of them, he stopped moving but kept barking.

"Get away!" Chloe shouted, clearly rattled by the dog.

Jackson came around the corner. He seemed almost surprised at seeing Chloe and Darcy. He must have been following Smokey's lead. He drew his weapon and said something, but his words were unintelligible.

Darcy could guess at why his speech sounded so messed up. He'd likely suffered temporary deafness from the bomb blast. By her estimation, the bomb had been placed in the hallway and blown away part of the courtroom wall. Jackson had been standing very close to where the bomb had gone off.

Chloe laughed and dug the knife deeper into Darcy's throat. "Back off or she gets it." Chloe tilted her head toward Smokey. "And call your dog off."

Darcy tasted bile in her throat. The coppery scent of blood reached her nose and pain seized her neck. Chloe had made a cut in her neck deep enough to cause bleeding.

Jackson's expression changed. All the color left his face. His gaze fell on Darcy and then went to Chloe, who was now using Darcy as a full body shield. For Jackson to take Chloe out without risking Darcy's life, it would be an almost impossible shot.

The knife dug once again into Darcy's skin. The cut, however small, still stung. Based on everything she knew about the woman who held her at knifepoint, Darcy's best guess was that Chloe would slash her throat and then make a run for it, assuming that Jackson's focus would be on trying to save Darcy's life.

Would this be the last time she'd see Jackson? She mouthed the words *I love you*. It didn't matter if he felt the same way or not. She wanted him to know.

His expression showed that he'd understood though he did not say the words back to her.

Still holding the gun on Chloe, Jackson took a step forward, so that he was parallel with Smokey.

Chloe tightened her grip at Darcy's waist. "I said back off!"

Smokey watched Jackson, waiting for a command.

Jackson adjusted his grip on the gun. He tilted his head to the side, which must have been a command to Smokey because the dog started to bark aggressively as he advanced on Chloe. Definitely not something that was in the K-9 training manual.

"Call the dog off." Chloe took a step back, pulling Darcy with her, though the knife was no longer resting against Darcy's skin.

Darcy stepped on Chloe's toe and then elbowed her in the stomach. The move was enough that she could get away. Chloe turned and ran. Smokey was right on her heels.

Jackson returned his gun to its holster and took off after her. Darcy fell into a run behind them. When she looked up the street, she could no longer see Chloe or Smokey, and Jackson had disappeared down a side street.

The smart thing for Darcy to do would be to find help. Jackson probably couldn't use his radio because his voice was so hard to understand. She ran back toward front of the courthouse, where she was likely to find another police officer.

As she ran, she caught a flash of movement one street over. Chloe running. Chloe must have made an about-face and was heading back to hide in the crowds of people affected by the chaos.

Darcy bolted up one block, thinking she might be able to cut Chloe off, but that plan would only work if Jackson came up on Chloe from the other side. Darcy had no weapon and Chloe had a knife and was stronger than she was. Maybe that wasn't such a good idea.

Darcy sprinted toward where she'd seen Chloe and pressed against the side of the building before peering out. She caught just a glimpse of Chloe as she turned another corner. Darcy looked the other way as Jackson and Smokey approached.

"She's going to try to hide in the crowd again." Darcy looked right at Jackson so he could read her lips. She wasn't sure if he understood her or not.

Jackson pulled his radio off his shoulder and touched his ears indicating he still couldn't hear very well. Darcy clicked the radio on and spoke into it.

"Attention all Brooklyn K-9 Units and patrol officers in the area. I'm Darcy Fields, speaking for Officer Jackson Davison. Chloe Cleaves is in the area surrounding the front of the courthouse. She is wearing a blond wig, but she might ditch that, and has on workout clothes—all dark colors."

Tyler came on the radio. "Darcy, what's going on with Jackson?"

"He has temporary deafness."

"We'll be on the lookout for Chloe, but we

are sort of all-hands-on-deck at this point dealing with injured people."

Several other officers also responded that they had gotten the message and would search as much as they could.

Jackson reattached his radio to his shoulder and they both ran back toward the crowd. They slowed as they drew closer.

She could be anywhere.

"Maybe we should split up," Darcy said.

Jackson shook his head and then tugged on her sleeve. His gaze went to the outer circle of the crowd first. Chloe would probably try to escape before the mayhem died down.

All the faces were starting to look alike…

Please, God, don't let her get away again.

They drew a little closer to the crowd outside the courthouse. Darcy was losing hope.

Smokey took off running even though Jackson hadn't commanded him to do anything. The dog raced toward an EMT and tackled her. The woman was wearing a baseball hat and a vest that identified her as an EMT.

Jackson ran after Smokey. Darcy followed.

The EMT was Chloe.

She scrambled to her feet and turned to run.

Smokey lunged at her again, this time hanging on to the hem of her vest.

Jackson aimed his gun.

"Hands up! You're under arrest!" Darcy shouted.

Jackson gave her a raised-eyebrow look.

Darcy shrugged. "You can't talk very well, and I've always wanted to say that."

Chloe broke free of the vest. She whirled around, slicing the knife through the air at the K-9. Smokey backed up but started in again with his aggressive barking.

Jackson bellowed something that sounded a little bit like *"Back off"* as he ran toward Chloe, firing a warning shot into the air. Chloe put her hands up.

Knowing that Jackson's words weren't going to make a lot of sense, Darcy moved in. "Drop the knife, Chloe. It's over."

Chloe let the knife fall to the ground.

Jackson used a hand motion to direct Smokey to sit and stop barking.

"At least the trial got interrupted," Chloe said.

"I'm sure they will reschedule," Darcy returned. "Due to extenuating circumstances."

Within minutes, they were able to lead Chloe to a patrol car.

As the car drove away, Darcy felt like she could finally take in a deep breath and relax. It was over.

She grabbed Jackson's sleeve and looked

into his eyes. "Jackson, I meant it when I mouthed the words 'I love you.' It wasn't just because I thought Chloe was going to kill me."

He nodded in understanding and then mouthed the words *I love you, too.*

He gathered Darcy into his arms, kissed her and then held her. She rested her face against his chest, breathing in the scent of his skin as her heart filled with joy.

Smokey whined at their feet. They both laughed and knelt to pet the Lab.

EPILOGUE

The next day, Jackson waited at headquarters for Darcy to come by. As soon as Chloe had been taken into custody, Reuben had pled guilty and turned on her. Numerous charges, including attempted murder, had been filed against the woman. Both offenders were going to be locked up for a long time.

Jackson felt both tense and excited for what he had planned when Darcy arrived in about an hour. He was still on duty, so she'd agreed to meet him, thinking they were going to walk to Sal's for lunch. He had something much bigger planned. He'd bought a scarf for Darcy that looked like something she would wear, all bright and colorful. He looked down to where his K-9 sat at his feet. The scarf looked good tied around Smokey's neck.

Penny McGregor sat behind the front desk, tapping away on her keyboard.

She lifted her hands from the keyboard.

Jackson looked over at her. Her face had drained of color. On a pale-skinned redhead, it made her look almost like she was coming down with the flu.

Jackson sensed the shift in mood. "Everything okay?" He stepped toward her.

She rested her hand on her chest. "I just got a threatening email. The source is anonymous, but since we know Randall Gage killed my parents, it must be from him."

Jackson knew some of the K-9 Unit was actively searching for Gage, whose DNA had been found at the crime scene. It had taken twenty years to get that DNA, but now that they knew the killer's identity, he was still eluding justice. They had to find Randall Gage.

Several other members of the team, including Bradley, Penelope's brother, had just entered the reception area.

"What is it, Penny?" Bradley asked. "What does it say?"

She read from the screen. "'It was a mistake to let you live…you first, then your brother.'"

A tense silence invaded the room.

Gavin, who had been among the team members to enter the reception area, spoke up. "I don't want either of you to worry. We're going to catch Randall Gage."

"I know you will," Penny said. She glanced

nervously over at her brother before returning to work.

"Forward that email to me," Gavin said. "We might be able to figure out where it originated from."

"I'll do that." Penny's jaw tightened. She was still clearly upset.

Bradley walked over to her and patted her shoulder. "We will catch him." Jackson caught the promise in the detective's expression before he disappeared down a hallway along with the other officers.

Jackson offered her a reassuring nod. "We'll make sure he is put behind bars."

"I know everybody has my back and Bradley's," Penny said. "That doesn't mean messages like this don't make me afraid."

"Understood," Jackson said.

The unit got back to work. Threats, even those that hit very close to home, were unfortunately a routine part of their day as law-enforcement officers. They would get Randall Gage—and the killer of Lucy Emery's parents. Jackson had no doubt.

His phone dinged. Finally. It was a text from Darcy saying she was two minutes away. Jackson thought it best to meet her outside. He wanted the moment to be somewhat private.

He stepped outside with Smokey just as Darcy got out of a taxi. She waved at him.

"This is it, buddy," Jackson said.

Smokey wagged his tail.

Darcy came toward him. Her eyes were bright and clear. "It's good to be back at work."

"Yeah, now life can get back to normal for both of us." Though he managed to look and sound calm, Jackson's heart was pounding.

Darcy looked over at Smokey. "Nice scarf."

"Actually, it's for you. Smokey just wanted to try it on."

She laughed.

"Go ahead. Let's see how it looks on you."

She knelt to untie the scarf.

Jackson had twisted it to hide the surprise inside. He waited in anticipation as Darcy flattened the scarf. A ring fell on the concrete.

Darcy stared at it for a long moment before picking it up. "What's this?"

Jackson got down on his knee, took the ring and held it up. "Darcy, I love being your friend, but I would like to be your best friend for the rest of your life. Will you marry me?"

Darcy let out a light breath. "Oh, Jackson. Yes, I will marry you."

He placed the engagement ring on her finger as she looked into his eyes.

Smokey licked her cheek and they both laughed.

Jackson rose and held his hands out to her. She stood. The look of love in her eyes warmed his heart. He leaned in and kissed her.

Behind him, the entire K-9 Unit broke into applause.

Penny smiled. "I saw what was going on out the window and called the team over. When it was clear she said yes, we came outside. I'm glad something good like this happened today."

Considering the threatening email Penelope had received an hour ago, the gesture of support touched his heart.

Jackson spoke to Darcy. "Sorry, I wanted it to be a little more private."

"It's okay. They are sort like family anyway," Darcy said.

He gathered her into his arms and joy filled his heart. Smokey let out a little bark of approval and sat at their feet looking up at them.

* * * * *

*Look for Tyler Walker and
Penelope MacGregor's story,*
Cold Case Pursuit,
*by Dana Mentink, the next book in the
True Blue K-9 Unit: Brooklyn series,
available in October 2020.*

*True Blue K-9 Unit: Brooklyn
These police officers fight for justice with
the help of their brave canine partners.*

Dear Reader,

Thank you for taking the journey toward love with Jackson and Darcy. I'm sure, as a reader, the level of danger they faced created some nail-biter moments for you. I know it did for me as I wrote some of those scenes.

Both Jackson and Darcy had been burned in past romantic relationships. They had to learn how to open their hearts and trust again. And they needed discernment to know that their relationship was different from the ones in the past. It might not be with a romantic relationship, but each of us has a choice to make and each of us is affected by past hurts and bad experiences. Yet we can't remain stuck or give in to bitterness.

My prayer for myself and for you the reader is that you will trust God and see each situation with clarity. Not an easy task. Just like Darcy and Jackson had to not let the past define their future, we have to do the same.

Sharon Dunn